PUT THE PLEASURE
BACK IN
YOUR READING

Do your eyes get tired easily? Do you hate reading paperbacks because of the crowded gray pages?

LARGER TYPE
MAKES THE
DIFFERENCE

PUT PLEASURE IN YOUR READING
Larger type makes the difference
This EASY EYE Edition is set in large, clear type—at least 30 percent larger than usual. It is printed on non-glare paper for better contrast and less eye-strain.

FOG HIDES THE FURY

PAULA MINTON

PRESTIGE EASY EYE BOOKS
PRESTIGE BOOKS • NEW YORK

FOG HIDES THE FURY

PRESTIGE BOOKS INC. • 18 EAST 41ST STREET
NEW YORK, N.Y. 10017

Chapter
ONE

I REMEMBER, when I was a little girl, that I read Carl Sandberg's poem about the fog. I know that I always remembered it, especially that phrase of how it comes on "little cat feet," because the words were so simple, yet so graphic. Yet when I was a child, the fog of San Francisco did not really have much meaning in my life, except in my fancies. Oh, I suppose like any other child I was accustomed to it, as I was to the breathtaking orange and red and purple of the setting sun out by Cliff House, where the avenues end, or the reassuring sight of the lofty spans of the Golden Gate Bridge. I think that when you are very young, you think that the world has been created just for you. So you take for granted all the phenomena, and they become a part of the decor and the pattern of your days without your being really aware of any one of them.

I think I was more afraid of thunder and lightning in those days than I ever was of fog, and there are not many electrical storms in San Francisco. I was afraid, too, of the rumbling tremors of the occasional earthquakes that have always plagued San Francisco because of its location on the San Andreas fault. Of course, it was more than a generation before I was born that the City by the Golden Gate was destroyed by earthquake and fire, but I remember the terrifying tremors of March 1957 and how the floor had swayed under my feet at noon; and then at seven in the evening, when I had been lying down before going out to dinner with Aunt Clara, there was another violent shock that nearly threw me onto the floor.

No, fog was my friend and my ally when I was a child, and I would pretend that I could be a fairy princess and summon my mantle of invisibility to cloak me and hide me from unfriendly eyes. I didn't have many playmates then, and so I was fond of that game. It was an escape, of course. I had only to pretend, if I had been naughty and Aunt Clara had scolded me for some tiny peccadillo, that I could snap my fingers and suddenly the gray strands of fog would begin to curl around my body in a strange and mystical garment. And once the garment was completed, only those whom I loved and whom I wished to see me could see me. I must have borrowed that fanciful notion from Edna St. Vincent Millay's poem "The Harp-Weaver," I know now, for I was very fond of poetry as a child, and my father had many books in the big library of the old house on Telegraph Hill.

It is said that a London fog is the thickest and

most engulfing. Others hold for the Maine fog, off Kennebunkport, where the damp northeast wind drives clouds of fog before it. Still others speak of the fogs that grandiosely sweep into the majestic fjords of the Scandinavian countries. I cannot tell, for I have been to none of those places. I have spent all my life—and I am nearly twenty-one —here in the city of my birth, in San Francisco, where my parents themselves were born.

Sometimes, depending on the winds and the tides of the Pacific Ocean, you will see fog in the downtown streets of San Francisco on an otherwise cheery morning. But usually it begins about four in the afternoon, as foreboding clouds begin to roll in from Seal Rock, stretching along the Great Highway out as far as Pacifica, and then advancing through the maze of Golden Gate Park and downward to the city and to the landmark of Coit Tower. Sometimes it is capricious and hides only a part of the forty-nine square miles that comprise what the famous columnist Herb Caen has named "Baghdad-by-the-Bay."

One thinks romantically of Chinatown, of the exotic little shops and the restaurants along Grant Avenue, some of them with their Chinese symbols in multicolored neon lights dimmed by the thick nocturnal fog. One thinks of the warfare of the tongs, of the pungent smell of joss sticks and the more insidious smell of opium, as Chinatown must have been in the days when San Francisco was famous for its brawling, bawdy Barbary

Coast. But the fog is so indigenous to San Francisco that today only the tourists really seem to notice it and to complain about it.

But I am not so sure any longer that fog is my friend and my ally as it was when I was a child.

I was an only child, but I know that I was very much loved by my father and mother. I know, too, that my father told me, the day before my seventh birthday, when I naïvely told him that I would love to have a baby brother for my birthday present, "Darling, we'd like nothing better either. But it's God's wish that you're to be the only child we shall ever have, so I'm afraid I can't give you your birthday wish." And later, of course, Aunt Clara —who was Mother's sister—explained that Mother was extremely delicate and had nearly died in childbirth having me, and the doctor had said that she couldn't have any more children. My parents' names were Amy and Wilson Dade, and they named me Arlene after my father's younger sister, who died of scarlet fever when she was only thirteen.

I'm sure my life would have been different if I'd had brothers and sisters, but as I have said, mine certainly wasn't an unhappy childhood. Yes, it was more introspective, and of course it was lonelier. But by way of compensation, my father and mother spent a good deal of time with me. My father was vice-president of the Dade Navigation Company, which had its offices at the foot of

Market Street in the old Ferry Building. His father, who had held the same post, had brought him into the firm right after his graduation from San Francisco State College and had put him to work first as a dock hand unloading freight from the many cargo ships that were part of the large Dade commercial fleet. My mother had been his college sweetheart, with aspirations toward becoming an artist. Aunt Clara still has some of Mother's watercolors and the original manuscript of an unfinished book of poetry, some of the verses of which were printed in *Argonaut* magazine and in the San Francisco *Chronicle*.

Both my father and mother loved good books, music, the companionship of a select group of friends. And though I was only a little girl, they shared these pleasures with me. My father had a huge library of poetry, art books, excellent fiction, and autobiographies, and I still remember many a foggy winter evening when he would take me on his knee in the big overstuffed armchair in the library and read to me. Often he would stop, and then the two of us would discuss what he had read, so that he could always be sure that I understood it. And he and Mother often took me to the symphony or to the opera at the War Memorial Opera House on Van Ness Avenue. There was an old Chickering grand piano in the wide, ornately furnished living room, and sometimes Mother would play Chopin and Mozart while my father and I sat and listened, his arm around me, his blue eyes twinkling, his firm mouth giving me a quick, affectionate smile every so often when I recognized one of my favorite passages and squirmed about with excited pleasure.

Yes, it was a happy childhood, full of imagination and fantasies and illusions. And the old house on Union Street, one of the very few that had survived the great 1906 earthquake and fire, was like our own very special castle, shutting out the rest of the world, a haven against the darkness and the thick fog that crept in from the ocean. When we heard the mournful foghorns from the direction of Alcatraz Island, I would pretend that the armies of our foe were marching toward our castle to lay siege to it. And I would snuggle closer to my father and think of how, if by some artful means they should break into our castle, I could summon my invisible cloak and hide from them, and hide my mother and my father, too, until the danger was past.

And that was how it was until just a month before my eleventh birthday, when they were driving home across the old narrow wooden San Mateo Bridge after visiting one of Mother's closest friends. It had been raining nearly all day, and a heavy fog had settled over the Bay area just before dinnertime as they were on their way home. I remember that I had had a slight cold, and so I hadn't gone along with them. Aunt Clara had come over to look after me until they got back. And then they hadn't come and hadn't come, and about eight o'clock the telephone had rung and Aunt Clara had answered it, and I had heard her say, "Oh, my God!" and then begin to cry. And a few minutes later she had come back into the living room and had taken me in her arms and told me what had happened.

Some driver coming in the opposite direction, ignoring the hazardous driving conditions and the lighted signs that forbade a speed of more than thirty miles an hour, had come at them with blazing headlights, and my father had been blinded and swerved directly into the path of the oncoming car. All three of them had been killed instantly.

That was the first time I knew that the fog was not always my friend. It was not to be the last.

Chapter
TWO

I'VE SAID that things had been just the same during my childhood till the month before my eleventh birthday, when Mother and Father were killed. That wasn't really quite accurate, because just two weeks before my parents died, they'd unexpectedly decided to rent out the old house on Union Street and take the top floor of an attractive new duplex out on Forty-fifth Avenue, only a few short miles from Cliff House and Seal Rock and the ocean.

I remember that my father called Mr. Murray, the lawyer who worked for him and handled some of the tax and corporate matters of the Dade Navigation Company. I'd been sitting in the living room reading while my father was talking on the phone in the hallway just outside, and I'd heard him say that it was high time he and Mother got away from the gloomy house on Telegraph Hill and out where there were more light and trees and a view for Mom and me to enjoy. And a few days later my father had driven us out to the new apartment, and the next day the moving van had brought our furniture and our clothes, and Aunt Clara had come over that same evening to cook our first dinner in our new home.

Then I remember how pleased my parents looked at having left the house where they'd begun their marriage and where I'd been born. Indeed, they had seemed younger and gayer that evening than I could remember having seen them before, except maybe during the holidays, when they went out of their way to entertain me. The old house had become very familiar to me, of course, with all its narrow passageways and its attic and its mysterious basement, which I never had quite thoroughly explored. Perhaps that was why, I just couldn't accept suddenly changing to a brand-new apartment with newly painted green walls and an artificial little iron balcony just outside the living-room window in a building that was right up against another in the long row of buildings that looked exactly alike all down the street. Of course, Golden Gate Park was only a few blocks away, and Aunt Clara did take me walking there of an afternoon, though we never really went beyond the boundary of Lincoln Way, which ran east and west. Aunt Clara used to say that it was dangerous to go deep into the park even in broad daylight and that a little girl could get lost there.

And then, of course, just two weeks later, when my parents were killed, I could think only of the old house and how things had been for me with the two of them there, growing up with them and being happy even if I didn't have a baby brother or even a baby sister. And Aunt Clara would join us at least once a week for dinner, and sometimes she would take my mother and me out to dinner if my father had to work late at the office.

After my parents' death, Aunt Clara was my only living relative. Her full name was Clara Harwood. She had never married, and I recall that when I was a child I once overheard her say something to Mother about "once hurt, twice shy." I didn't find out what she meant until I was almost through high school.

She was about five years older than my mother and, though not quite so good-looking, attractive in a pleasant sort of way. She had dark brown hair, as I do, and she wore it close in a prim, tight bun at the back of the neck, combed away from the forehead and parted down the middle. Her face was round, her lips rather thin, and she had my mother's delicately aquiline nose, high forehead, and delightfully dainty ears set close against the head. Where Mother's eyes were widely spaced and large and hazel, Aunt Clara's were a mild blue with very short lashes. Before she became my guardian, she lived in a small apartment over on Lombard Avenue near Van Ness.

Laurence Harwood, Mother's and Aunt Clara's father, had been the head of a prosperous San Francisco investment firm, and he had left both of them a great deal of money when he died, a few years before I was born. So Aunt Clara had never really had to work for a living, though she kept herself occupied with volunteer campaigning to raise funds for the opera and symphony and was a Gray Lady at the La Honda Home for the Aged. She was also something of an expert dressmaker and seamstress, with a flair for original design. Every so often, when she felt in the mood, she would visit one of the exclusive fashion salons on Geary or Powell, shut herself up in her apartment for a week or two, and then come over to show Mother the sketch for a new frock or slipover she'd designed.

All things considered, she was good-natured, loyal, and very devoted to me. Her only sometimes irksome habit—which, of course, I discovered only a few years ago—was her distrust of men. She was also a chronic sufferer from asthma, which she seemed to have contracted when she was hardly out of her teens. Mother had often gently chided her about continuing to live in San Francisco, with its fog and dampness, which surely didn't help her condition. But Aunt Clara loved the city where she'd been born and always sniffed and said, "I'd much rather suffer from asthma and live here than have perfect health in a noisy, insufferably crowded place like New York or Chicago."

I could understand her prejudice in favor of her birthplace, because I felt exactly as she did. There are many things I like about San Francisco, things I discovered when I was a child. The breathtaking view from Twin Peaks at night, when you can see the entire city spread out before you in multicolored panorama, and think up fanciful stories about the people who live way over there just to the left of that tiny blinking green neon light. The cable car running up California Avenue, with all its passengers joking with the gripman as if all of them belonged to the same big, friendly family. I still remember how I used to envy the nonchalant way in which a man would jump off, when the cable car came near his stop, and keep on walking, hardly losing a step. Aunt Clara would have spanked me soundly if I had ever tried that stunt, but how I wanted to do it! And I loved to walk through Chinatown and see the strange herbs and foodstuffs displayed in the windows of tiny shops, the exciting arrays of wonderfully patterned and alluringly colored gowns and fans on view in the department store at the corner of Grant and Sacramento. To walk along where Taylor Street ends and on down to Fisherman's Wharf and then the Embarcadero.

I remember—and you can still see it today, for that matter—just off Taylor Street, the crowds of tourists and the stands where you could buy freshly baked loaves of sourdough French bread and live crabs in big buckets. And you could go into a quaint little shop near DiMaggio's and stand there for hours staring at the tables where they displayed sea shells from all over the world. And I remember the stately elegance of the Mark Hopkins and Fairmont hotels facing each other atop one of the city's steepest hills. And the smell of chocolate coming from the old brick building of the Ghiradelli Candy Company, which faced a little strip of beach where you could wade. Indeed, unless you drove way out to the end of the city at the ocean, where broad beaches stretched all the way to Pacifica, you really didn't have any other place to wade or swim. And even there wading was an adventure, because the temperature of the water seemed to be in the low forties the year around.

These and so many other things that I recall are changing now that I have practically come of age. For example, now there's a mall down at Ghiradelli Square with all sorts of shops and amusing little restaurants. And where many of the stately old houses pressed together like good neighbors afraid to part for a moment, high-rise apartment buildings are going up. But they still have the sour-dough French bread and the crabs and that heavenly Mrs. See's candy (which you can't find in any of the other forty-nine states, unless, of course, you order it by mail). So, as you can see, I shared Aunt Clara's views pretty much.

It took me a long time, though, to get used to the new apartment and to being without my parents. Aunt Clara gave up her apartment and moved into the duplex so that she could take care of me on a full-time basis. Then it was a somewhat different life, because of course, there wasn't the wonderful companionship my parents always gave me. Aunt Clara wasn't quite so fond of books and music as they had been, so naturally I missed being read to or listening to music and discussing it.

Now that I was living out on the Avenues so near the ocean, I was made more aware of the fog than I had been in the old house on Union Street. Because most of the time, about five o'clock in the evening, it began to roll in from just about where Aunt Clara and I were living. And it was thicker, and there was more wind driving it, because way out there there were fewer buildings to stand as bastions against the wind that carried in the clouds of gray, rolling mist and made mile upon mile of apartments and houses into a city of ghosts and eerie shadows.

Chapter
THREE

AT THE TIME of my parents' death, I was going to John Muir Grammar School, which had been conveniently near our house on Telegraph Hill. Aunt Clara, seeing that I liked the school and had many friends there, saw no reason for having me transferred to one that would be closer to our apartment out on the Avenues. She owned a Ford sedan and drove me to school every morning and back home every afternoon, except on those days when she was busy with her charitable and social duties. On such occasions, she had me take a cab. My schoolmates naturally looked upon this chauffering service as a mark of my considerable financial status. Children can be devastatingly candid and cruel toward anyone they suspect of being a nonconformist, and so the subject of my being driven to John Muir in style and having either a taxi or Aunt Clara's car waiting for me at the curb when I left school soon became a fascinating topic for conversation.

All at once, after the death of my mother and father, I discovered that some of the boys and girls

I had liked best became my most malicious critics. Often, when I was walking down the corridor from one classroom to another, some of them would say in a loud voice that I was certain to hear, "Arlene must have had lots of money left her. She doesn't walk home or take the bus, she gets picked up and sometimes she even goes home in a cab all by herself. It must be lots of fun to be so important!" And Mary Frances Carter, who had been my very best girlfriend ever since my first day at John Muir, openly chose as her new best friend the girl who sat next to me in class. One afternoon, as we were leaving the classroom, Mary Frances said to her new friend, whose name was Jane Busby, glancing back at me to make sure I knew the remark was intended for me, "You know, Janie, I just can't stand stuck-up kids!"

I remember that on that particular afternoon, Aunt Clara had gone to a fund-raising luncheon for the symphony. As was her custom, she herself had placed an order for a cab to be waiting outside the school when I came out. But what Mary Frances had said to Jane Busby had made me so upset and so unhappy that I marched straight past the cab and up to the corner, where I waited for a bus to take me all the way out to where we lived. And when I got home, I went to my room, flung myself down on the bed, and cried like a baby.

I couldn't see that I had changed at all, because

I still tried to be just as friendly with my classmates as I always had been. The effort was useless—they just wouldn't accept me as they had in the old days. And then one day, when I just couldn't stand their snubbing me any more, I went up to Mary Frances Carter and told her that I wanted to know just why she was treating me as if I was dirt. That's when I found out that I was what the story books call a "wealthy heiress." Because Mary Frances just giggled and said to me, "Treat you like dirt, Arlene? Oh my gosh, I wouldn't dream of doing that. Not to somebody who's going to come into half a million dollars someday. I'm just scared to talk to you at all because you're so important. And my father is only the assistant manager of a hotel you probably wouldn't even think of staying at."

"You're hateful, Mary Frances!" I burst out, trying hard not to show the tears that were misting my eyes. "I haven't got any money, and besides, even if I had, it wouldn't make any difference. We used to get along so nice last term, and now all of a sudden you're mad at me."

And then Mary Frances had just giggled again and said, "If there's anything I can't stand, it's liars. Don't you know we kids read the newspapers too, and not just the comics? And when your folks got killed, there was a story about how much money was put away in the bank for you till you got to be twenty-one? My gosh, that must be almost all the money there is. Anyway, I like Janie better now anyway." And then she had given another one of those dirty giggles of hers and walked away.

So that night, when Aunt Clara was preparing supper, I tried to find out if what Mary Frances had said was really true. And I told Aunt Clara how nasty the kids had been to me in school ever since Mother and Father had died, and then I told her what Mary Frances had said to me that afternoon. Aunt Clara had been stirring a pot of stew —she was a very good cook, and she often prepared meals just for the two of us—and she stopped and turned to me and said, "I'm sorry you had to learn it that way, Arlene. Yes, it is true. You're much too young now to know what all that money means, and Mr. Murray, your father's lawyer, is in charge of it till you come of age. There is a trust fund for you till you come into all your money, and it will see you through college. But I felt that it was my duty to bring you up just like any other normal child, without pampering you or letting you feel that because you had money to inherit, you were any better than anybody else."

"I don't feel better than anybody else, Aunt Clara!" I sobbed. "I haven't done anything to them, and I still like them just the way I always did!"

"Someday, dear," she told me, "you'll discover that people judge you by how much money you have in the bank, by your address, by the clothes you wear and your social background. It's not fair,

I agree, but that's the way it is with a lot of people. Unfortunately, you had to find it out before you're really old enough to understand it. Do you want to leave John Muir and go to a private school?"

I shook my head as the tears rolled down my cheeks. "No, I don't, Aunt Clara. I'm going to try my best to make them like me the way they used to. I don't ask them about their parents or how much money they have in the bank. Why should they care about what I'm supposed to have? Because I'd rather have Mummy and Daddy back than all the money there ever was in the whole wide world!"

Aunt Clara dabbed at her eyes with her handkerchief, then picked me up in her arms and hugged me and kissed me. "You poor darling," she said, "I know you would. I know how much you miss them, and it can't be very pleasant for you cooped up with your stuffy old aunt all the time."

"Don't say that, Aunt Clara," I protested as I returned her kiss and hug. "You aren't old and you aren't stuffy, and I love you a lot."

Aunt Clara turned back to the stove, and I heard her sniffle. "This asthma of mine is getting me all choked up. Now you go wash up for supper, Arlene, and we won't talk about the kids at school any more, will we? You're going to show them that you're just the same nice little girl you always have been, and you're going to do well in class and make me proud of you, and pretty soon they'll come around and find out how silly they were not to keep you as a friend." She turned her head again to give me a comforting smile, then added, with a flash of her inimitably wry humor, "I baked a chocolate cake this afternoon, and you're going to get an extra-large piece for the nice things you just said about me. But of course, they aren't really accurate, darling. I'm thirty-seven years old, and I'm what is referred to as an old maid. But thank you anyway for trying to improve my morale."

That was the first time that Aunt Clara had ever hinted at the unhappy love affair that decided her on remaining a spinster and that was to motivate her in watching over me vigilantly so that I didn't run the risk of a similar heartbreak.

For the rest of the time that I was in grammar school, I insisted that I be allowed to come home by myself on the bus in the afternoon. I even wanted to go that way in the morning, but Aunt Clara wouldn't hear of it, so we compromised on having her let me out of the car a few blocks away from school so that my classmates wouldn't see me being "chauffered." I ignored their cutting remarks and went on with my schoolwork and tried to act as if nothing had changed, and by the time I was fourteen and ready for high school, I had won back some of my former chums. But because my marks were exceptionally good, a lot of the others accused me of being a teacher's pet and a goody-goody. Mary Frances Carter was one of those.

High school was different. Aunt Clara sent me to Galileo, and all the kids were very grown up and had more diversified interests like sports and dating and going to the Blackhawk to sip cokes and listen to Dizzy Gillespie and Miles Davis play their exciting brand of jazz. At fourteen and a half I was changing, too, from the gawky child I had been in grammar school. In those early days, to make matters even worse, I had had to wear braces on my teeth. By the time I entered Galileo, thank goodness, I had outgrown them

I liked my teachers and my classmates, and I particularly liked Mrs. Wilding, my English litera-ture teacher. I had the advantage, of course, of reading fine books from my father's library and having been read to by my parents, and I found that Mrs. Wilding had in her adult way a great zest for discovering a fine book and communicating it to the class. Because I was still very lonely, living with only Aunt Clara and having to start all over again at high school to try to make new friends, I took refuge in the world of books. I remember being full of youthful ideals and burning indigna-tion over injustice and bigotry and prejudice. I read John Steinbeck's *The Grapes of Wrath* and Dostoevski's *Crime and Punishment* and Thomas Hardy's *Tess of the D'Urbervilles* and *Jude the Obscure*, and their characters were as real as living persons. Mrs. Wilding, seeing how enthusiastic I was, gave me special assignments, like writing themes about what my favorite books were and why I particularly liked them. And she encouraged me to read even more mature books that weren't actually part of the curriculum.

But what I liked best about Mrs. Wilding was that she could see how hard I was trying not to try to call attention to myself just because of my love for schoolwork and the books I was assigned to read. The first week of class, indeed, she called me aside one afternoon and had a little chat with me. Before I knew it, I had managed to tell her— without really being aware that I was doing so— the problems I had had at John Muir. So, though she gave me extra work and extra themes, she didn't call the attention of the class to my grades or to the excellence of my themes. She put a grade on them and returned them to me, usually with a little note hidden inside the sheaf of pages, so that I could read it by myself when no one was looking. And I was deeply grateful to her. Also, discovering that I had to make less of an issue to make good in school as a kind of defense against the loneliness I had experienced the last few years at John Muir, I could become less self-centered and begin to enjoy companionship and the everyday routine of growing up.

I think perhaps relating my experiences now after they have happened can be very definitely traced to the influence of Mrs. Wilding. I'm only sorry that she'll never have a chance to read this, because she died just before Christmas last year. But at least I had the chance of telling her, on graduation day at Galileo, how grateful I was to her for all her kindness and inspiration.

As I said, I began to take more of an interest in my classmates because they seemed to accept me, and I didn't encounter the treatment that Mary Frances Carter had dished out to me back in grammar school. Just a few weeks after my sixteenth birthday, one of the boys in Mrs. Wilding's class asked me to go out with him on a soda-and-movie date on a Friday evening. He was a very popular boy, a senior, towheaded, strapping, and always in good spirits, a passable student—and quite a baseball and football player, from what the girls told me. His name was Johnny Linden. I shall always remember his name out of sentiment; he was the very first member of the opposite sex to show a personal interest in me as a girl and to disregard my scholastic ability or my financial standing. And if this sounds cynical, remember that Aunt Clara was beginning to sermonize constantly on the subject of not being taken in by the male species.

Naturally I told her about Johnny Linden's asking me out. Aunt Clara frowned and said it was high time she had a talk with me, and she turned a bit red in the face. I suspected what she was going to tell me, and I'd already read enough from my biology textbook to save her the trouble and embarrassment, so I said as much.

"Arlene, I wasn't about to suggest that you were going to have an affair with this boy," she retorted, "but I know how unhappy you were back in grammar school because the children were snubbing you. And you were terribly introspective. That was understandable. But now you're getting along better in school, and you want to have the friends and the good times you see your classmates have."

"That's exactly right, Aunt Clara."

"Well, I'm for that too, dear, but discreetly. Because, you see, deny it as you will, the fact still remains that you're Arlene Dade, the heiress to a considerable sum of money and a good share of the Dade Navigation Company stock when you come of age five years from now. If—just for the sake of argument—you should go out with a boy and maybe he'd have an accident with the car or take you to a place that got raided—well, you see, dear."

"Oh, for heaven's sake, Aunt Clara!" I burst out. "And if I walked in front of a car and didn't watch where I was going, I could get killed. That's silly."

"It's not at all the same thing, Arlene, and you know it. You're an extremely intelligent girl, even precocious, and I can tell the signs in you of wanting to kick up your heels and just be happy-go-lucky and do what all the other young people are

28

doing. But you can't. You've your background to remember. And if you don't, I assure you other people will. Newspaper reporters and columnists. Do you remember my reading to you last month that item in Herb Caen's column in the *Chronicle* about a certain black sheep of a family who sneaked away from the clan in Sacramento to paint San Francisco red?"

"Yes, I do. But what's that go to to do with my having a date with Johnny Linden?" I wanted to know.

"Only that I happen to know that young man mentioned in the column. His family has its headquarters in Sacramento, and they own a dozen radio and television stations and almost as many newspapers. He was being groomed—he's a cousin to the husband and wife who own the controlling interests of that big chain—to go into a very responsible position at one of the television stations and work his way up to a very important job someday. But he wanted to have some fun, and a few years ago he came up here by himself and went on what we might politely call a binge. The newspapers printed a story about it. Ever since then, he's like a remittance man—you remember that story of Somerset Maugham's. The family pays him an allowance every year on condition that he stay away from Sacramento for good. And he's had to change his name. That's just one example of how the wrong kind of publicity can hurt a person, Arlene dear."

29

"All right, I understand what you're trying to tell me, Aunt Clara," I answered patiently. "And I think I'm a pretty good judge of character for my age, and I don't think Johnny Linden is going to be a remittance man or black sheep or anything like that. Now, may I go out with him or may I not, Aunt Clara?"

She sighed, took me by the hand, and led me over to the living-room couch. "I guess it's time for me to tell you a story, Arlene dear."

"Why, you're not going to give me a lecture on you-know-what, are you?"

"Arlene Dade! Really, sometimes you exasperate me!"

Aunt Clara had a worried look on her attractive face. "I'm terribly conscious of the fact that I do not have the inclination for books and music the way your poor father and mother did, because you may rest assured I would have seen to it that I selected your reading material. Why, when I was sixteen I still thought that the stork brought babies."

I was about to be flippant, but the hurt look in her timid blue eyes made me think better of it. After all, you don't go out of your way to offend the only relative you've got, especially when she's your guardian and a very nice aunt into the bargain. So I just looked quizzically at her and waited for her to tell me what she wanted to say.

"Why then," she continued, somewhat mollified by my sudden subdued manner, "maybe you'll understand me better, dear. Maybe you'll understand why I'm so concerned about everything you do from now on, now that you've come to the adolescent stage of your life, which is the hardest time of all for a girl. Yes, yes, we won't discuss sex. We'll take it for granted that you know the elementary facts about it. But that's all you know. I'm not going to embarrass you by asking you if you had any puppy-love crushes on any of the boys at school—even this Johnny Linden—because I respect your intelligence and common sense. Only, at your age, Arlene, it's very easy for a girl to be carried away by feelings she can't control, especially if the boy is unscrupulous. And when I was nineteen, I made a dreadful mistake because I thought I was grown-up and capable of knowing what a person's character really was."

"I don't want to pry, Aunt Clara," I put in then, because she was averting her gaze and her cheeks were somewhat flushed.

"No, no, I have to tell you. It's important that you understand such things so that you can profit from the experience of others. You see, Arlene, my father left both your mother and me a lot of money from his own business. Your mother was smart enough to let Father's lawyer keep it in trust and invest it wisely. So when she married your father, she had more than when she started—and it's part of the money that you're going to inherit when you're twenty-one. But I wasn't thinking of the future and investing money and dull things like that—I wanted to have a good time and to travel and to feel that I was young and fresh and, well, not too unattractive."

"I told you you're still very good-looking, and I mean it," I tried to help out. But she wasn't listening to me. She had a faraway look in her eyes, and she was still holding my hand. I felt the convulsive grip of her fingers as she drew a deep breath and went on with her story.

"Well, Arlene, Father's lawyer—his name was Davis Jenner—always seemed to show me a little partiality. I don't know why. Anyhow, I told him that I wanted to draw just enough money out of my trust fund for a trip to South America. I had always wanted to see Rio and Buenos Aires, and Mother and Father had no objection, because they were going to Hawaii to celebrate their wedding anniversary. Your mother had to take some special courses at school that summer to get ready for high school, so everything worked out just fine. Father was always of the opinion that we had been brought up well enough to know our station in life and to be able to make our own decisions, and he felt the trip would be very good for me."

"It must have been thrilling for you, Aunt Clara," I mused. "I've seen color slides of Rio, and I envy you having been there."

"Oh, yes, it was beautiful enough and I was very proud of myself because I spoke a little Spanish, and I had made all the arrangements for my hotel and the trip on the boat myself. I had my whole itinerary worked out. Only at the hotel where I was staying, there was a handsome young mining engineer from San Diego. He was going down the Amazon to do some exploratory testing for his company. He was about twenty-seven, six feet tall, blond, and terribly good-looking."

I felt Aunt Clara's fingers tighten convulsively on my wrist and heard her sigh nostalgically. "Well, to make a long story short, Arlene, we fell in love. That is, I thought he did, just as I did."

"How terribly romantic!" I exclaimed.

But Aunt Clara shook her head. "That's what I thought too, dear. But Norman Calloway—that was his name—had other ideas. He told me that he had signed a five-year contract with his company and that he would be away from civilization all that time. And he said that now he had met me and fallen in love with me, he couldn't bear the idea of hiding away in the South American jungle and maybe having me find some other man and be lost to him forever."

"He sounds like the knight in shining armor out of a storybook, Aunt Clara."

She gave a mocking little laugh. "You see? If this Johnny Linden handed you a line like that— to use the atrociously vulgar jargon of your generation, Arlene—you'd think exactly that. Just as I did. Yes, I fell for that line. He proposed to me and he said that he was going to tear up his contract and cable his employers that he wouldn't accept the job. And so . . . well, I let him make love to me."

I pretended not to look at her, because I knew how embarrassed she was at having to talk so frankly to me. I just said a little "Oh" and looked down at the floor. And then she said, her voice cold and bitter as I had never heard it before, "And then after our few weeks of paradise on earth, I found the serpent. The serpent was the conniving young mining engineer himself. He had a friend back in San Francisco, and he had cabled him to get all the financial information he could about me and my family. And he found out that I was an heiress and it would be much more profitable for him to marry into the Harwood money than to take that five-year contract."

"How dreadful, Aunt Clara! But how did you ever find it out?"

Aunt Clara really blushed this time, gave me a sidelong look out of the corner of her eye, then said, very matter-of-factly, "Because by that time we were sharing the same suite and he'd been in town shopping for a present for me. I came in earlier than he that afternoon, and the clerk handed me the cable answering his. I suppose it was a perfectly natural mistake, and it certainly was a blessing in disguise for me. Because as soon as I got upstairs and opened it and found out that his friend had told him to a penny what I was worth, I wrote a note and attached it to the cable and

34

then I took the next boat for home. I never saw him again."

"Didn't he ever try to get in touch with you again and explain things?" I pursued.

Aunt Clara shook her head. "No, I'll give him credit for that, anyway. My note made it very clear that I never wanted to see him again, and I told him exactly what I thought of him."

She looked at me, and now there were tears in her eyes. "Now you know something I never even told Amy—your poor mother, darling. And now you know why I'm so strict with you. I don't want any heartbreaker like Norman Calloway to come into your life as he came into mine."

And that's why, the next morning at school, I told Johnny Linden that I was awfully sorry I couldn't keep our date.

Chapter FOUR

AFTER MY GRADUATION as valedictorian from Galileo High School, Aunt Clara gave me a reward of a trip to Hawaii, sailing on the S.S. *Lurline*. We spent a week in Honolulu at the lovely Reef Towers, with a lovely air-conditioned kitchenette apartment with a lanai balcony looking out toward Waikiki Beach and the serene blue Pacific. We watched surfing at Makaha Beach, where the waves hurtle up to a dizzying twenty-foot height and browsed in all the exotic shops. Sometimes we ate at the Willows, a house and estate whose owner turned it into a wonderful tropical garden, with a terrace for diners right over a fishpond into which you could drop tidbits and watch carp and crabs and ducks fighting for their share. Aunt Clara liked French cuisine, so we dined also at Michel's at the Colony Surf, as well as at the Floating Pagoda Restaurant and Canlis' Charcoal Broiler.

We spent another heavenly week touring the islands of Maui, Molokai, and Kauai, and, of course, the big island of Hawaii itself. I thought the people were the friendliest I had ever met, and the lovely, lazy atmosphere and the color and the good food and the breathtaking scenery made me think that someday, if I ever got married, I would want to come back and maybe stay all summer. It was certainly every bit as romantic as what I had read about Rio or Buenos Aires or even Rome or Paris. Needless to say, I did not mention my impression to Aunt Clara, not after the story of her own heartbreak. The way she had reacted to my wanting to date Johnny Linden, as well as her candid announcement that she intended to be strict with me whenever I wanted to have a date with a boy, was forewarning for the future. Looking back now, maybe the reason I fell in love with Alan Caswell was as a kind of subconscious protest against Aunt Clara's eternal distrust of handsome men. But I am getting ahead of myself.

All told, we spent an unforgettable month in the islands, and even Aunt Clara seemed to relax and to be much more flexible as a companion. In a way, it was like taking a traveling finishing-school course just going along with her, because she gave me many suggestions about how to dress and behave in public, what foods to order (I wasn't yet at the age when I was allowed to order a vintage wine!), and all the little amenities that, to use her own words, "a potential heiress ought to know really by instinct."

We got back about the middle of August, and I prepared to enter San Francisco State College.

Because of my scholastic standing at Galileo, I was gratified to learn that a partial scholarship would be offered to me. Aunt Clara, who admitted to Scottish ancestry several generations back, was delighted at this unexpected dividend for my having applied myself so diligently in high school. "It's an old maxim, dear," she informed me, "that people of means stay that way because they are not extravagant and because they take advantage of opportunities. Just the same, that scholarship award, gratifying as I know it is to you, also makes me feel that the way I've brought you up couldn't have been entirely off the beam, so to speak." Aunt Clara had a habit, somewhat disconcerting at times, of mixing the most formal language with popular slang expressions. I think maybe she wanted to show that in spite of being a "lonely old maid" (as she occasionally referred to herself when she was feeling particularly out of sorts or in a mood for sympathy), she had as youthful an outlook as I.

However, I couldn't help twitting her right then and there by reminding her that the Dade Navigation Company owned one steamship that carried passengers to the Orient and stopped off at Honolulu. She gave me a sharp look and rejoined, "I am perfectly well aware of that, Arlene. However, if you are going to have any voice in the management of the company when you come of age, you ought to know what your competition is. Besides, the *Lurline* specializes entirely on the Hawaiian cruise, while the *Asturia*" (the name of our ship) "features the trip to Japan and stops at Honolulu only to pick up cargo and additional passengers." It was apparent that Aunt Clara was a particularly level-headed and clever woman, and I am sure she was hoping that I'd assimilate enough of her own outlook to save myself many a headache later on. Of course, when you're very young, as I was then, you have a habit of being a little bit impatient toward your elders, because sometimes you think you know exactly what they are going to say before they say it, and you're convinced that it won't be the right answer anyway. Or at least, that it won't be the answer you would have made. Just the same, I loved her very much, and I only hoped that she really knew how I felt about her in spite of her occasional "intellectual arguments."

But the plain fact was that I really didn't care about taking any active part in the steamship business. Yes, I knew that when I became twenty-one I'd have a controlling amount of stock in the company, but Aunt Clara had told me that it was being run very efficiently by a general manager by the name of Henry Pitt and a commercial sales manager named William Pearson. Both of them had been with the company over twenty years, and they were certain to know the intricacies of the business.

Besides, I had already decided what I wanted to do when I got out of school—to be a schoolteacher. I think my decision was based on the enjoyment I had had all through grammar and high school of coping with intellectual problems, with delving into fascinating books, whose characters were as real to me as the people I saw on the street, and with having worked under such inspiring teachers as Mrs. Wilding. I can remember how she would sit at her desk, just as she was ready to plunge us into a new book adventure, perhaps Melville's *Moby Dick*, and her lips would form an eager little smile and her dark blue eyes would begin to sparkle with enthusiasm as she started to tell us something about the author and the importance of his book. And before she had finished that preamble, I felt almost impatient; I wanted to have the book right then and there and begin reading it. That was how she affected me, because she was a really great teacher. And what was more, I wasn't the only one who thought so; almost everybody in her class used to say how glad they were they'd taken English lit, because it wasn't at all dull, as they'd been afraid it might be.

That was one main reason I wanted to be a teacher, of course. Perhaps, too, I thought of being able to work with young people at a time when they would be most impressionable and have the most enthusiasm for taking hold of values and applying them to their own lives. That was the way I had felt in school. Yes, I'll admit that I turned to books after my parents' death as a kind of escape, but I think it was more than that, really. Anyway, for any of the reasons I thought I had, that was why I planned to take four years of college, get a certificate, and then see how well I could work with children. I wanted to have a class not with the youngest kids, but starting about the age of Mary Frances Carter. Maybe subconsciously I thought that if I found someone just like her in my class, I could change her outlook so that she wouldn't be a snob or catty or nasty the way she'd been to me.

San Francisco State College had a really beautiful campus on Holloway Avenue, not far from southwest-suburban Westlake. They had a fine music department, and they gave student concerts at which many famous professional artists appeared. They also had a very good drama department. I decided I wanted to try out as an actress, because it would mean understanding the moods and feelings of others, and that would be very good preparation for being a teacher. And that was where I had my first real "crush" of what Aunt Clara would have called "puppy-love," when I met Jim Kinsolving.

Chapter
FIVE

I was seventeen and a half years old when I entered San Francisco State College in the fall, just after Aunt Clara and I had enjoyed that wonderful trip to Hawaii. Naturally, having had that trip made me feel considerably more mature than my age, and, as I'd always thought, the students at the college were quite a different group even from what I had found in high school. They were generally much more serious, and though they still had fun and dates and all that sort of thing, most of them were there for an education to prepare them for a career later on. So if you were a thoroughly industrious and dependable person, you could expect to make friends, and I did.

Although Aunt Clara had always emphasized that I was an heiress and that I should therefore take more pains to cultivate the "right sort of people" and not make friends too readily, I never did really agree with her. I knew how miserable I had been in grammar school because of the barrier that had been put around me when my classmates found out about my parents and the money I was going to inherit someday. They treated me as if I'd been a freak. In high school, I mixed a good deal more, even if Aunt Clara still didn't let me date, but in college, I was resolved to make more friends and be less self-centered than ever. Now I could appreciate and sympathize with Aunt Clara's wariness when it came to getting romantically entangled. Just the same, I thought it was only good common sense to know as much about people as I could, so that if I ever really had to make any decisions in the steamship company, I could be a better judge of character and human nature.

These, then, were the reasons I enrolled in the drama department as an optional course during my freshman year. However, they had a rule that I wasn't allowed to do any real work in that class, since it only had about a half credit, until I had shown satisfactory grades in the first semester. By the time Christmas vacation came, I'd registered high marks in all my classes, and so there wasn't any objection to my adding an hour on a Thursday afternoon to see if I had any talent as a potential actress.

It was a kind of workshop, not like Professor Baker's famous Yale Workshop, where students read their own plays and had them produced and criticized by their own classmates as well as by Professor Baker himself, but rather one of those "learn by doing" groups. I've always had a feeling that college ought to be something like Antioch or Berea, where you learn the schoolbook rules six months of the year and then go out and hold a job and try them out for size the rest of the time. That way, you don't just get by because you've got a good retentive memory or a facility for cramming. You've got practical experience, and you can weigh and judge what you've learned and whether it works out in everyday life.

We had about thirty-five students in what they called Drama I, and the assistant head of the department, Wilmer Creston, was in charge of us young theatrical hopefuls. There were about twenty girls to fifteen boys. Of course, that caused a little intense rivalry, because if the play we were going to produce happened to have more important roles for men, we girls felt slighted, and vice versa. Wilmer Creston was six feet tall, about thirty, jovial and witty and rather good-looking, even if he did wear glasses. But he had a boyish look of enthusiasm to him and a flair for making tired old warhorses like *Tartuffe* or *La Dame aux Camilias* come to life. His method was something like that of the French teacher I had had in high school, who suggested that we take a novel or a play, delegate ourselves a certain section of the novel or a specific role in the play, study all we could about the economic and political and cultural history of the period of that book or play, and then either do a term paper on the book or present a class play in the assembly hall by way of a final exam. I thought it was a wonderful idea,

44

and I know that I learned more French than if I'd sat there studying the past preterite subjunctive, which is used only in poetry and oratory.

By February, a month away from my eighteenth birthday, we were preparing *Romeo and Juliet*, under Professor Creston's direction. Three other girls besides myself had read for the part of Juliet, and Professor Creston had chosen Laura Anson as the lead and me as her understudy, which was very flattering. Out of the fellows in our group, Jim Kinsolving was the most talented and also the best-looking. He was nineteen, a sophomore, with curly black hair, candid blue eyes, a frank, smiling mouth, and the build of an athlete. He happened to be on the second team in football, which was one reason he had such poise and grace on the stage. Also he had a fine, resonant baritone voice that could be toned to the youthful quality Professor Creston wanted for the character of Romeo.

From the social viewpoint, I'm quite sure that Jim Kinsolving wouldn't have caused Aunt Clara any alarm. He was the younger son in a family of two boys and three girls, and his father was Donald Kinsolving, the well-known patent attorney. His mother had been a social belle who made her debut at a formal coming-out party at the Mark Hopkins Hotel, and she herself was a descendant of one of San Francisco's oldest families. And they had plenty of money in their own right. So even if

I had got really serious with Jim Kinsolving, I don't think that Aunt Clara could have written him off as just another fortune hunter.

We were to put on *Romeo and Juliet* about the middle of March on a Saturday afternoon in the school auditorium. A week before the performance, Laura Anson came down with a bad attack of laryngitis, so I was called upon for the dress rehearsal. Memorizing lines was no problem at all for me, because my high marks throughout school had come about through a retentive memory. You either have it or you don't, and I was lucky.

Jim Kinsolving and I hadn't really been much more than casual acquaintances. He being a sophomore, his schedule was naturally different from mine. I really don't think he'd noticed me especially, but here we were at the dress rehearsal, I wearing the attractive dress that the star, Laura Anson, was due to wear at the performance a week away, and he was a fine, strapping Romeo. I've always wondered how Shakespeare really intended Juliet to be played, particularly since he described her as being fourteen years old and yet gave her a womanly wisdom and an intense awareness of both physical and spiritual love, which you certainly don't find in most fourteen-year-old girls these days. I didn't want to play her as a saucy little coquette nor heavily enough to suggest that she was a mature young woman, so I strove for the happy medium. There was just enough flirtatiousness to her, combined with a real desire for love, I felt. Professor Creston didn't correct my delivery much during the dress rehearsal, and then we came to a dialogue between Romeo and Juliet in Act I scene 5.

ROMEO: If I profane with my unworthiest hand,
This holy shrine, the gentle sign is this—
My lips, two blushing pilgrims, ready stand
To smooth that rough touch, with a tender kiss. . . .
JULIET: Saints do not move, though grant for prayers' sake.
ROMEO: Then move not, while my prayer's effect I take:
Thus from my lips, by yours, my sin is purg'd.

I knew that at the end of this speech, Romeo kisses Juliet, but I wasn't prepared for the reality. And then Jim Kinsolving's hands were on my shoulders, firmly holding me, and his mouth was on mine, just briefly.

"No, no, Jim!" Professor Creston called as he rose from his seat. "That's the way you might kiss your mother-in-law." Of course, that got a laugh from everyone and eased some of the tension of the dress rehearsal. "This is the girl you love, Jim. You don't have much opportunity to see her, and you've got to make every moment count. Put all your heart and soul into that kiss, because you remember that Romeo speaks of the kiss as purging his sin through prayer. Try it again now. Arlene, go back to the 'Good pilgrim, you do wrong it,' and let's have it sustained now."

So I repeated my lines, looking up at Jim, who was taller than I, of course, and we smiled at each other as if to say "Hello" for the first time, and then he was kissing me again. And this time his fingers tightened on my shoulders, and his lips, firm and warm, lingered on mine just long enough to make me conscious of what it was to be kissed by a most eligible male.

Color stained my cheeks, and I felt my knees trembling under me. I hesitated a moment, groping for my lines. "Then had my lips the sin they have took," until a titter ran through the rest of the class.

Professor Creston quipped, "Well, that certainly was much more effective. You seem to have stunned our Juliet into forgetting her lines," and that drew an appreciative and prolonged laugh.

I managed to acquit myself ably enough during the rest of the play, and I tried not to overdramatize the death scene. At the end, Professor Creston remarked that all of us had shown a good deal of talent and industry and enough imagination to make the formal presentation quite worthwhile. There was going to be a final rehearsal the Friday before the performance. We walked off the stage, and Jim Kinsolving followed me. "Excuse me, Miss Dade," he said as we were going back to our seats. "I hope I didn't embarrass you up there."

"Of course you didn't. And please, the name's Arlene."

"Good. I like that much better. And you can call me Jim."

The upshot of it was that when we finished the dress rehearsal, Jim Kinsolving asked me for a date for Saturday night. Now I happened to know that Aunt Clara was going to the symphony, and so for once in my life I decided to make my own decision without consulting her. I said yes. Jim proposed to take me to Grison's Steak House for dinner and then to see Gwen Verdon in *Damn Yankees*, an extremely popular musical that was the hit of the town. Aunt Clara didn't care for baseball, and unfortunately the musical was all about baseball, so I knew that she probably wouldn't ever have taken me, but I wanted to see Gwen Verdon, because she was such an irresistible comedienne, and she could dance like an angel.

Jim and I got along just fine at dinner, and by the time our dessert came along, we felt as if we had known each other for years. He was going to go on to law school and take his bar exam and go into his father's firm if he passed it.

I purposely tried to be a good listener, and I said as little about myself as possible, except to ask him if he didn't have a steady girl. That was just by way of making conversation, but it sort of rebounded like a boomerang, because Jim looked at me with an odd little smile, then said, "Oh, sure, I've dated around, Arlene. But I think I'd like you to be my steady girl."

"When did you get that idea?" I wanted to know.

"This afternoon when I was kissing you," he came right back at me. He was candid enough and honest, and I admired that. So I said I would.

I hadn't told Aunt Clara about my going out with a young man on Saturday night. I'd told her that I was going over to the college to brush up on my lines for next week's performance since there was more than an outside chance that I might take Laura Anson's place as Juliet. Well, I got away with it that time, and the next week too, when I had a date on Friday evening with Jim. Aunt Clara had to go over to Sausalito because the women fund raisers for the opera were holding a semiannual dinner and a meeting in that colorful and Bohemian little hamlet just beyond the Golden Gate Bridge.

For our second date, Jim and I had dinner at the Fairmont and then danced to the music of Ernie Heckscher's great band. I wore an off-the-shoulder blue formal dress that Aunt Clara had bought for me after my graduation from Galileo, and I felt very daring with my throat and shoulders bare. I was glad that I had a clear, smooth complexion, especially when I noticed Jim glancing at me every so often. The music and the good

50

food and his companionship had put me into a mellow mood, and I suppose both of us were going through a kind of idealistic stage at that point in our lives. Anyway, during one very lovely waltz, he danced me toward a darkened corner and then kissed me on the mouth again, whispering, "This isn't part of the play, Arlene. This is because I want to kiss you. You're gorgeous tonight. When you see somebody every day in class, you get used to them, but tonight it's as if you were an entirely, wonderfully different girl."

I blushed with becoming maidenly modesty, but I didn't feel modest, because that kiss of his had awakened emotions against which Aunt Clara had warned me. I knew that because I had been so sheltered all my life, it would be awfully easy to fall in love with Jim Kinsolving. And I told myself that I ought to find out what love is all about, entirely on my own. No, I promised myself I wouldn't make the same mistake Aunt Clara had made. This was a different generation, and all of us knew more—or at least thought we did.

Well, without going too much into the details, I can say only that by the time June rolled around and my freshman year was over, I'd managed to escape Aunt Clara's vigilant supervision enough to have a dozen or more dates with Jim Kinsolving. And then one evening just after college ended for the summer, when Aunt Clara was off to another of her incessant board meetings, Jim Kinsolving drove me in his Thunderbird out to his parents' summer home, a lovely cottage in Muir Woods, which is past Sausalito and a retreat for craftspeople and artists and wealthy retired persons.

That night I let him make love to me, because I wanted to know what it was really like and because I was very fond of Jim Kinsolving. I even thought I might marry him.

I wasn't disappointed. Young though he was, Jim was extremely considerate and very gentle with me. And of course, theoretically I knew enough not to make the intiation an awkward and distressing one for him. I think we both enjoyed the experience, and I know that we both exchanged rhapsodic pledges for the future and agreed to be "unofficially engaged," as the saying has it.

I don't know whether we both would have fulfilled that pledge, but we never did get a chance to find out if our clandestine little affair could have been nurtured into a happy and lasting marriage. Because Jim Kinsolving suddenly decided to enlist in the army that August, and three months later I read in the newspapers that he was killed in Vietnam.

And so I had my own secret of an unfulfilled love, like Aunt Clara's. The only difference was, I never told her. And to this day I have no guilty conscience about having deceived her or about my own conduct. It was a normal and natural thing for both of us to have fallen partly in love. You can say that it was fate that kept it from being any more than that. And of course, if it hadn't been ordained that Jim Kinsolving and I should never marry, there'd be no further story for me to write.

Chapter
SIX

AFTER Jim Kinsolving's death, I tried to absorb myself entirely in my studies at San Francisco State College. For one thing, if I'd shown any emotional crisis Aunt Clara might have suspected that I'd become involved with a man, and a great deal more intimately than she could have imagined. There was simply no point in needlessly upsetting her. I went on with the drama group, and Professor Creston was especially helpful and understanding that next fall, because he'd admired Jim as a fine, well-balanced person who had a capacity for getting along with people and meeting the strenuous physical demands of an athlete and at the same time demonstrating a marked ability in scholarship and in the fine arts. Jim Kinsolving had been a completely rounded individual, and even today I can remember him with admiration and sorrow at the shocking termination of his life just as it was beginning. I think he would have been very good for me, because he had both imagination and common sense.

There isn't much to say about the rest of my

college career, except that I managed to keep out of what Aunt Clara would call "trouble with a capital *T*." In my junior year, I played the lead in Ibsen's *Hedda Gabler* and, the week before I was graduated at the end of this January, that of Portia in *The Merchant of Venice*. Professor Creston congratulated me on the convincing rendition I gave these roles, and Aunt Clara was there in the front row to applaud me when the curtain fell and to have a messenger come onstage to hand me a bouquet of flowers. I noticed with some amusement that the floral bouquet was twice as large as the one she had awarded me in my junior year. She had always such a perfect sense of proportion, did Aunt Clara.

My marks were good, a high B average all through the four years, and in my senior term I'd taken a special course in geopolitics at Aunt Clara's suggestion. She thought that since I was coming of age and would be concerned with the affairs of the Dade Navigation Company even in a minor role, I ought to know what was going on in the world and how the Cold War struggle for power might affect the company whose principal stockholder I would become. On the evening following graduation ceremonies, Aunt Clara arranged a dinner in my honor at The Blue Fox, one of San Francisco's swankiest restaurants. She invited Douglas Murray, who had been my father's attorney and who continued to act as executor in my behalf.

Douglas Murray was fifty-one, tall, wiry, with a brisk military bearing coupled with a charmingly suave personality. It was the first time I had met him since Aunt Clara had taken me to his office just after my parents' death. Ten years hadn't changed him much, apart from adding a good deal of gray to his neatly cut black hair—it wasn't far from being a crewcut, doubtless to make him look younger. I'm quite aware that men are sometimes as vain as women when it comes to appearance and age. But I liked him, because he treated me without any hypocritical deference, though of course, at the graduation dinner very little about the estate was discussed. He was simply there as a pleasant companion, a close friend of the family; and Aunt Clara's purpose in inviting him, of course, was to remind him that my twenty-first birthday was only a few months away.

It was a wonderful dinner, and I think that what I remember most about it was that finally Aunt Clara allowed me to select wine because I was practically of age. When I chose a Clos de Beze 1959 with my filet mignon, she nodded approvingly and remarked to Mr. Murray, "You'll find, Douglas, that my niece has acquired an excellent education that is practical as well as theoretical. Her marks have been exceptionally good, and she's been particularly practical in selecting courses that will give her some insight into the state of the world these days, so that she won't just be a mere coupon clipper in the company."

Douglas Murray lifted his wine glass and toasted me, and I looked properly demure and grateful. "Well, Miss Dade," he formally addressed me, "I look forward to meeting you in my office on your twenty-first birthday, and we'll go into specifics. But for now, let me congratulate you on having matriculated from college and for being such a prepossessing young woman. I've a sneaking suspicion you're going to be one of the most popular heiresses in San Francisco."

"I'm sure you do, Douglas," Aunt Clara retorted dryly, "but that's not exactly to her credit. You know perfectly well that even an ugly shrew would be popular if it were known that she was to come into a fortune in cash and the controlling stock of a very prosperous steamship company. I trust, Douglas, that you will handle the press with your usual acumen and try to give out as little data as possible of the kind that would make these scandalmongers who pass as reporters believe that they've found another Lola Montez."

"I hardly think that Miss Dade in any way resembles that notorious though beautiful creature —not, I hasten to add, that Miss Dade isn't quite as beautiful—but there's simply no comparison when it comes to background and good sense," Douglas Murray riposted gallantly. Again I demurely lowered my eyes and took a sip of my wine and tried to pretend that the two of them weren't "buttering me up" for their own personal reasons.

I could understand that Aunt Clara was somewhat proud of having fulfilled her role as guardian, and justifiably so. I could also understand that Douglas Murray intended to remain the official lawyer for the Dade estate and, knowing that I would have something to say about it rather soon, wanted to ingratiate himself with me. But I also quite agreed with Aunt Clara as regards newspaper publicity about my coming of age. I certainly had no desire to be bothered by fortune hunters and still less to be looked upon as some glass-caged freak for the curious to ogle and to envy simply because through the accident of birth I was to find myself independently wealthy. Thanks to Aunt Clara, I had a thoroughly sensible notion of the value of money, and I had never really been extravagant as a teenager even knowing in advance that I could afford any whim so far as travel and clothes and fine restaurants and the theater and the like were concerned. My theory was that if I didn't try to spend it all right away, there'd be enough left in later life when I might really want it.

And so, on the twenty-second day of March of this year, I found myself sitting in Douglas Murray's office, with Aunt Clara beside me, and Mr. Edmund Husing—the senior partner of Douglas Murray's law firm—there to preside over the official reading of the will as it pertained to my inheritance as the only surviving heir of Amy and Wilson Dade. Spring starts in February in San Francisco, and this, my most important brithday, was on one of the loveliest, sunniest days of the entire year. Even that evening, as if the elements had been conspiring to celebrate my birthday, there was not the slightest trace of fog. Perhaps that was a good omen. Or, perhaps too, it was a way of allaying all my secret anxieties about what future weighty obligations were to be thrust upon me. . . .

Douglas Murray began by congratulating me on having attained my twenty-first birthday and thereby legally coming of age as the sole heir under the terms of my father's will, with the exception of a substantial bequest for Aunt Clara. He took the will from a file folder lying on top of his desk, put on a pair of spectacles, and quickly glanced through it before beginning to read it aloud. The gist of it was that I was now to come into full possession of the trust fund that had been set up with Aunt Clara as my guardian, in addition to which I was to receive the conveyance from Mr. Murray—who was also the legal representative of the Dade Navigation Company—of seven hundred fifty shares of preferred stock in the company. Aunt Clara had been left a hundred fifty, and the general manager, Henry Pitt, and the sales manager, William Pearson, were each to receive fifty shares.

"You understand, Arlene"—Mr. Murray took off his glasses and gave me a friendly smile—"the terms of this will initially gave you and your mother equal holdings in both the trust fund and the company stock. The proviso under which you claim your mother's share was, regrettably, added by your father at my own suggestion in the event that by any unforeseen chance, both he and your mother should predecease you. And it is under the terms of this proviso that you legally inherit what I have just stated."

"May I ask a question, Mr. Murray?"

"Of course, Miss Dade," he replied. "It is our earnest hope that we may continue to serve you as we were privileged to serve your father."

"Yes, yes, of course. I'm quite satisfied about that," I said. "But what you've just told me about the stock means that for all practical purposes I'm the owner of the company. Is that true?"

He glanced at Edmund Husing, who himself answered my question. "Yes, Miss Dade, that is the fact of the matter. Your father, however, did make the further stipulation that before you made any drastic changes or even considered putting up the Dade Navigation Company for sale, that you consult with Mr. Pitt and Mr. Pearson, in view of their long service and devotion to the company and their obviously greater experience in the business."

"Of course I shall," I replied. "And if the company is doing well, I certainly would have no intention of selling it."

"There is one thing more, Miss Dade," Douglas Murray continued. "You also are to inherit the

Dade house on Union Street, by the terms of the will as modified by the existing proviso which I have already mentioned to you. Your father added a codicil shortly before his death, to the effect that it was his wish that upon attaining your twenty-first birthday you take up residence in this house. As your aunt has probably told you, just before his death your father instructed me to arrange for the rental of that house, and for these past years we have had a quite satisfactory tenant in the family of Edward MacIntyre, who operates a very prosperous automobile dealership on Van Ness Avenue. We have already served prior notice on Mr. MacIntyre, a few months before your coming of age, and he and his family have already moved to a house on Twin Peaks. The house is in excellent order, I may say, having personally inspected it myself only last week, and I am happy at this time to turn over the keys to you."

He opened a drawer of his desk, took out a key ring with four keys on it, and walked over to my chair to hand it to me. "There are duplicates to the front door, Miss Dade, one to the cellar, and one to the back door, which looks out into the garden. I think you'll find them in order. I might add that the rentals which this office has been collecting from the MacIntyres have been progressively credited to the estate, minus necessary expenditures for repairs, decorating, and the like. Our accountant has prepared a tabulated analysis of your holdings as they stand at the present date, and the money itself, of course, has been deposited with the Bank of America, as have the shares of preferred stock in their safety deposit vault in your name."

Aunt Clara looked at me with a little smile and nodded encouragement. Needless to say, I was just a bit dazed; even if you've been told for the past few years that you're going to come into half a million dollars in cash and the control of a thriving company, you still aren't emotionally prepared for it when it actually takes place. I found myself clenching my hand over the key ring with the four keys that opened the doors to the old house on Union Street, the house where I had played my little game of the fog's magic cloak and where I had felt so secure and happy as a child. Now it would have shadows of the past, the ghosts of my father and my mother. But they would be loving ghosts, and there was no need to fear their aura; it would be another kind of protective cloak to comfort me.

"I think that concludes the formal business of the day." Douglas Murray had returned to his desk, seated himself, and was smiling at me now. "Except that your father wanted you to know something about the history of the house whose keys I've just now given you."

"I'd like to know that very much, Mr. Murray."

"Well, it's certainly an interesting story, and it will give you some insight into how the company whose majority stockholder you now are came into being. Actually, the Dade Navigation Company was founded by your great grandfather Lorenzo Dade, who was born in London in eighteen forty-one, came to America with his parents a decade later, fought for the Union in the Civil War, and then came to San Francisco in eighteen sixty-six. He and a man named Philip Clarkson saw the possibility of hauling commercial cargo and fishing, and so they built two small schooners and soon had a thriving business going. Your great grandfather built the house on Union Street in eighteen seventy, on the occasion of his marriage to a young Boston schoolteacher by the name of Susan Eames, and eight years later your grandfather John was born. By that time, the Dade Navigation Company had a dozen or more schooners and fishing boats going as far as Baja California."

"I know very little about my grandfather, Mr. Murray. Father never really told me very much about him, except, of course, that my grandfather put him to work as a dockhand to start him out in the company right after he'd been graduated from the same college I went to."

"That's quite true, Miss Dade. But your grandfather John Dade was the man who really made the company grow, and his vision sent sailing ships to the Orient and to the islands of the Pacific ahead of any other commercial shipping firm. Indeed, he worked so hard that he didn't think of marriage until he was forty, and your father was born a year later. Your grandmother was a San

Francisco belle from an excellent family, but she died when your father was only three years old. The cause of death was a brain fever, so the old records tell us. Your grandfather, who loved her very dearly, was shocked by her tragically early death and plunged himself into work to try to distract himself. That effort, I may say, made the expansion of the Dade Navigation Company so energetic and farseeing that your own father's duties in the company proved to be mainly administrative. Your grandfather added merchant and passenger ships to the line and extended the ports of call to the Orient and the islands of the Pacific, as well as to Australia. He died, of course, five years before you were born."

"As I recall, Mr. Murray," Aunt Clara spoke up, "he committed suicide." I turned to look at her with surprise.

Douglas Murray nodded, found his spectacles on the desk, and toyed with them before answering. "That's true, Miss Harwood," he said at last. "John Dade was a man of Spartan endurance and self-discipline. He had actually been suffering a good deal for a few years prior to his death, but he refused to seek medical attention. When he was finally persuaded to do so, the cancer had spread beyond the hope of cure—and in those days, as you can well appreciate there was little hope even of arresting that dread disease in comparison with our own great progress in medical science. So, rather than prolong what he considered to be a needless and useless life, he shot himself. That was in nineteen forty, in the fall."

"And it took place in the old house, too," Aunt Clara again interposed, "in the library, from what Arlene's father told me."

Again Douglas Murray nodded. "Yes, one might say that the house on Union Street has had its dark hours. And your father, Miss Dade, who grew up there as a boy, knew what loneliness was."

This was another surprise to me, for Father had never referred to his childhood. "Your aunt," the attorney continued, "as your guardian and as one of the executors, has kept us apprised of your education and preparation for this important day. I know very well that you, too, had your lonely moments when you were going to grammar school, because your schoolmates thought you were on an elevated plane above them."

My face reddened, and I glanced somewhat irritatedly at Aunt Clara. That was all in the past, and there was no reason to bring it up again, I felt. But Douglas Murray was explaining. "You see, your father was brought up by a governess, a good-hearted German woman, herself a widow and childless, very devoted and industrious. But your grandfather insisted that she bring your father up with an awareness of his future station in life. He was kept from mingling with . . . well, to use an unfortunate term, commoners. The only friend he had as a boy was the little son of the caretaker of the house, who lived in a little flat a few

65

blocks away. And then, after your father finished college, as you know yourself, your grandfather put him to work as a dockhand so that he would not only learn the shipping business from the bottom up but also adapt himself to the people he would meet in every walk of life. It would have been better, of course, and certainly easier for your father, if John Dade had let your father mix more as a child. But that's beside the point. There's one final bit of history which you may find interesting, Miss Dade."

"I want to know everything I can about my parents and their forebears, Mr. Murray," I told him.

He put his spectacles back on and looked very solemnly at me. "Well, Miss Dade, besides being a hard worker, your grandfather John Dade was an inveterate gambler. About the time of the Spanish-American War, he put up the house as a stake in a poker game with Henry Caswell, who at the time had become a partner in the Dade Navigation Company. As it turned out, Caswell won the house. Remarkably enough, Caswell let your father live on there, charging him rent. Certainly a unique situation. However, a few years later, when fortunes changed, Henry Caswell fell into financial difficulties. The market had declined, and he himself had become grossly extravagant as regards high living. There were trips to Europe, there were"—he coughed politely—"other women, and to make a long story short, he sold the house back to your grandfather in an attempt to recoup some of his own lost fortune."

"Well," I said lightly, "you mustn't take me for a prim, unworldly girl who's been cloistered in a convent all her life, Mr. Murray. Those were the days of the Barbary Coast, and lots of unusual things happened. What happened to Mr. Caswell? There isn't a Caswell in the company now, is there?"

"Oh, no, Miss Dade. That rounds out my story so far as history goes, adding this one last piece of information. You know from your studies that San Francisco was razed by earthquake and fire in 1906. Well, the house on Union Street was damaged but not completely destroyed. Some of its foundation and a part of its structure were repaired and altered after the disaster. But at the time of that earthquake, Miss Dade, Henry Caswell, who had tried to corner the market again and suffered a second and final catastrophe, went to visit John Dade. From an old letter written by your grandfather to his attorney at the time, a letter which came into our possession years ago, he relates having received an angry note from Henry Caswell denouncing him for having robbed him."

"Robbed him?" I echoed.

"Well, Henry Caswell's financial losses had deranged his mind, I'm afraid. But he held your grandfather responsible, apparently, and he had written this threatening note saying that he intended to come and take retribution and to force

John Dade to share the fortune in jewels and gold which he knew your grandfather had hidden somewhere in the house on Union Street. But as Henry Caswell was making his way to the house on that morning of April 18, 1906, a few hours after the earthquake, he was struck and killed by falling timbers from a building nearby. That building, apparently, had been weakened by the terrible shock at dawn, and it was on the verge of collapsing when Henry Caswell chose that route to his appointment with your grandfather."

When Douglas Murray finished speaking, there was silence in the office. I sat digesting all that I had learned, and I couldn't help shivering. Yes, as Douglas Murray had just said, the old house on Union Street had known its dark hours. And now, in accordance with my father's express wish, I was to return to it. I wondered if the dark hours of the past were destined to return for me. I could not know then that there were to be many of them . . . hours when the shadows and the fog and the loneliness of the house itself were to conspire against my very life.

Chapter
SEVEN

AND SO, on the first day of April of this year, Aunt Clara and I moved back into the house at 777 Union Street, that period house so characteristic of the architecture of the turn of the century, when San Francisco was young and half-genteel, half-savage. From where it stood on Telegraph Hill, those who dwelt in the old house could see Coit Tower and the long, gradually turning span of the Bay Bridge, which connected Oakland with San Francisco. Almost at once, during the very first week of my return, I could recognize the difference in the foghorns that sounded around the Bay; they seemed to have a deeper-throated urgency than the ones I had heard from the apartment way out on the Avenues. And sometimes, when the wind blew a certain way, the fog coming in from the Embarcadero would be thicker and heavier and even darker than what swirled in from the Cliff House and Seal Rock. And once again I thought of my magic cloak. Perhaps, I told myself, I would need it more than ever now, for I was Arlene Dade, just turned twenty-one, a young, attractive heiress who could become the target for every scheming and ambitious eligible male that knew of my inheritance. I didn't like the feeling, of course, because I wanted to enjoy life and to go out and have fun and to meet people—the way I had done at college, which had really been the happiest time of my life up till now. But Aunt Clara, all that first week of our return to the house on Union Street, kept talking about my "new responsibilities and obligations to the family name."

The MacIntyre family had left the house in immaculate condition. I recognized at once many of the familiar pieces of furniture from my childhood—the big, overstuffed armchair in the library, the elegant Chippendale sideboard and buffet in the big dining room, with its massive drop-leaf walnut table at which twenty-four persons could comfortably be seated. And in the master bedroom on the first floor, the four-poster canopied bed which had been purchased by John Dade himself as the nuptial couch for himself and his young bride who was destined to die so soon after their union. The Oriental rugs in the living room and the heavy, beautifully upholstered davenport in front of the curtained bay window. The old stone fireplace directly opposite, with its ornate marble-topped mantelpiece, and the curiously shaped andirons with beautifully worked heads in the shape of bald eagles with spreading wings. John Dade had chosen this symbol of the eagle as his own insignia of success; he had sought to soar over his competitors in the shipping business, and I was back in the old house to prove that his dreams of a kind of empire had been realized two generations later.

San Francisco has always had a space problem; even today, with its forty-nine square miles and a good portion of that taken up by the army at the Presidio, you can stroll the streets and imagine yourself back in some old European town where one house is up against another and where the streets are narrow and the sidewalks narrower still. The house at 777 Union Street was imposing for depth and archaic elegance; yet it was flanked on each side by another house—though not so tall nor so imposing—in a way that should have made all the residents along the block feel hemmed in. Our house, like its two neighbors, was two stories high, but it towered above them in the addition of a severely peaked gable that gave the illusion of a third floor. Also, it was kept apart from its neighbors by an iron fence, taller than an average man, which completely squared it off at the back of the garden as along the sides and the front. At the front, there was a heavy gate, also of iron, and John Dade's symbol of the eagle rose from the center post of that gate. A heavy catch, which grated noisily when it was slid back—and this took strong pressure—allowed the resident or visitor to open it. As a child, I thought of that noisy catch as a kind of vigilant sentinel that would announce the arrival or departure of anyone. I remember that my father used to say that the catch was as good as a burglar alarm, because if a burglar sought to get into the house, the sharp-spiked tops of the fence bars all around it would inevitably make him try to come in by the gate, and then the noise would give him away.

The foundation of this old house had originally been of wide whitestone, which was grayish now. The house itself had been built of California redwood, chosen for its earthquake-resistant strength as well as its flexibility in yielding to those terrifying tremors. Nine wide, solid stone steps ascended to the porch, which was covered by an overhanging roof whose effect was to give the entire edifice the stately guise of a mansion. But this porch roof projected only over the doorway and not over the bay window of the vast living room. Stone colonnades supported it, rising at each side of the top of the steps. And the heavy oak front door was set well back of the broad living-room window, to achieve a further illusion of depth. Velvet drapes curtained this window, and I remembered that they had almost never been drawn aside. When my parents wished to enjoy the bright sunlight of an ideal San Francisco day, they retired to my father's study on the second floor directly over the living room, where there were two windows shaped with rounded arches; these were almost never curtained, except when the sun was excessively bright.

The roof of the old house was slanting, and it was dominated by the imposing gable above the study. From the street, one saw—or thought one saw—only the gable, for it was broad and towering like a third floor over its less aspiring neighbors on either side of it, and at the very top of the gable there rose a brass weathervane. Here again, John Dade's penchant for the eagle manifested itself, and the lordly bird gave even greater height to the house. If you live in a small town or in a city where the houses and the apartment buildings do not "rub elbows together," you may think that such a house as ours could not possibly provide privacy, and you would be wrong. So solidly had it been built that once the heavy oak door closed behind you and you stood within the hallway, with its oval-shaped handsomely scrolled walnut mirror hanging at one wall just above a small rectangular table and the hatrack and ornamental straightbacked leather-padded chair fronting the adjacent wall, you found yourself in a private world where only the sounds that came from within the house were audible to you. But since my parents had been fresh-air enthusiasts, they invariably left open a little window in the alcove next to the dining room, on the east side of the house, and through this window one could hear the sound of the heavy metal catch being drawn outside or clashing shut as someone entered or departed.

To the right as you entered, the foyer, or entrance hallway, led out to a narrow passageway that went past this alcove and into the dining room. Immediately to your left, the living room, with its arched doorway, beckoned. And straight ahead was an old winding staircase, with elegant finials and balusters and gleamingly polished handrails leading to the second floor. You could plainly see the landing, and I know that when I used to come home from school, sometimes Mother would be standing looking down at me with a smile of welcome and affection. And many times on such occasions both my father and my mother, smiling at each other with that secret pleasure in each other's company which a child does not quite understand but delights to behold, would greet me.

It was far too large a house for just the two of us, so Aunt Clara immediately engaged a young Irish girl named Rosie Murphy, who had been recommended to her by one of the women on the opera fund-raising board. Rosie had worked for this woman for two years and had left her situation only because her employer was remarrying and moving to her husband's house in San Rafael, where his own servants had been in residence for years. Rosie was about five years older than myself, industrious, pretty in a buxom, almost dowdy sort of way, and something of a Mrs. Malaprop with her attempts to use elegant phrases to hide her rather slangy everyday speech. I have a notion that Aunt Clara engaged her because Rosie had just broken up with her fiancé after a four-year engagement and had emphatically informed Aunt Clara that she had no use whatsoever for men. Perhaps Aunt Clara thought that adding her to our household would be a further deterrent to any nonsensical romantic notions I might entertain now that I was free, of legal age, and affluent enough to make the most of it.

Rosie Murphy proved herself to be an exceptionally good cook, and Aunt Clara gratefully ceded her own culinary skills in favor of Rosie's reasonably inspired efforts. Our neighbors on each side, the Portleys and the Randalls, employed a weatherbeaten, outspoken custodian by the name of Henry Jennings. He was a stocky, florid-faced bachelor in his early sixties whose proud boast was that he had cared for these houses as "maintenance supervisor" (one never uses the word "janitor" these days) for the past forty years. His speech was salty, and he was forever complaining about his arthritis, which San Francisco's damp evening air certainly did not benefit; but he was practically a mechanical genius when it came to improvising repairs, to getting balky furnaces working smoothly again, and to performing just about every onerous task that you yourself preferred not to do. It was Henry Jennings who first called my attention to the damp condition of the cellar a few days after Aunt Clara and I had moved back into the old house on Union Street.

After the 1906 earthquake, he explained, a part of the foundation had had to be replaced and with it a portion of the cellar. Whoever had done the work hadn't given much thought to hermetically sealed and leakproof construction, so that with a good substantial rain—as he so picturesquely put it—there was danger of seepage. "You'd best not store no clothes down there, Miss Dade." He gently shook his head at me. "They'd get mildewy overnight, I guarantee for sure. Now if I might be so bold as to suggest, Miss Dade, you let me order out a little cement and do some mixing and plastering myself, and I'll see if I can't stop it." So naturally I laughingly commended him for his solicitude in our behalf and told him to complete whatever repairs he felt necessary.

Later, I went down with him to see the cellar. I hadn't been very familiar with it as a child. There was a narrow wooden stairway from the back of the pantry, with a single and rather rickety guardrail, which led down to the landing. It was made of stone, with heavy columns and supports, and there was a locker room with wooden pickets enclosing it and letting you see just glimpses of some of the sheeted pieces of furniture, lamps, and bric-a-brac inside. They looked like ghosts waiting for night to fall so that they could assume their rightful shapes, I thought. I made a mental note to open the rusty old lock of that storeroom and investigate its hidden treasures, if any. Judging by the unusual assortment of furniture pieces in the house itself, I thought it quite likely that I might find a really genuine antique. John Dade's taste had been a mélange of rococo, pseudo-Gothic, and, incredibly enough, a fine Chippendale or Sheraton or Queen Anne piece which chastely denounced the garish ornamentation of little marble statuettes atop angular cherrywood or mahogany stands, a heavy and much too unaesthetic chandelier in the dining room, and tasteless (but very comfortable) monstrosities like that overstuffed armchair in the library.

Apparently, after the great earthquake of 1906, part of the cellar had been entirely sealed off by a solid wall of concrete. Yet the rest of it was spacious enough to let me think that one day I might have it remodeled into a recreation room. Of course, the ungainly but very serviceable furnace was in the way, as were some of the old water-pipes. Beyond the furnace, which was at the back of the cellar, there were three storage rooms, all made of the same wooden-picket style as the one I had first noticed. To one side was an old heavy wooden workbench on which lay rusty saws, hammers, and chisels. At the very back of the cellar there was a narrow stairway of about five stone steps leading to a narrow metal door. It was bolted and padlocked, and Henry Jennings informed me that he had possession of the old keys and would turn them over to me. The door led out to the garden, and here, if you could forget to look to either side of you and see the proximity of your neighbors' houses, you found yourself in a charming little sylvan setting.

On each side, along the tall wrought-iron fence, were beautifully compact and trimmed rows of hedges of flowering hibiscus and bougainvillea, one alternating with the other, yet an entire unbroken line in effect. The gardener had pruned them and shaped them into neat box-type sections. Then, at the very back of the garden and all along that side of the fence, there were rows of privet, those hardy evergreen shrubs with their compact, cheerful green leaves. Here and there were flowerbeds of gladioli, geraniums, and marigolds, each bed marked by a circle of decorative white pebbles. A winding cobblestone path made the tour of the garden, and in the center, flanked by four gingko trees, was a little white wooden summerhouse with ivy clinging along its trellises.

At the back and to the right was a huge stone birdbath in whose center stood a brass eagle, water trickling from its beak. From the screened porch, which was long but narrow, you could comfortably relax on the canopied swing and delight in the exquisite view, which was so completely your own. Along the sides of the porch, clambering ivy added its own picturesque note. And when the sun shone brightly on this garden, you could not believe that there was evil in the world nor shadows lurking anywhere to mar and distort the beauty of what you saw.

The garden had been exactly like that ever since

I had remembered from the earliest days of my childhood. The Saturday afternoon of our first week back in the old house, I complimented Henry Jennings on his artistry. To my surprise, he scratched his head and fidgeted about, then blurted out, "I'd sure like to take credit for all this, Miss Dade, but I rightfully can't. 'Course, I've kept it up fine the past twenty years or more, but it was my older brother Luke that worked the scheme out and had it put in for Mr. John Dade— that'd be your grandfather, now, wouldn't it?"

I nodded. "Yes; that's right, Mr. Jennings. But wasn't there always a garden, way back when the house was built?"

"I suppose so, ma'am. I know that Luke told Mr. John that the garden that used to be there wasn't really worthy of the house, and he talked your grandfather into letting him do the whole thing over again. That was back about nineteen twenty-two, as I recollect."

"Is your brother still alive?"

He shook his head. "No, ma'am. He died two years ago of the flu. He was seventy-four then. But I remember his little boy Gregory used to play in the garden with Mr. Wilson—your father, isn't that right, ma'am?"

So that was the caretaker's son who had been my father's only playmate and companion in his own lonely childhood, I told myself. "What became of your brother's son, Mr. Jennings?" I asked.

"Well, ma'am, just before the war, he figured there was more money to be made working at the shipyards than having a caretaker's job like his father and me. He'd got married by then—that was back in nineteen thirty-nine—and he and his wife had a boy. Both of them died last year in an airplane crash."

"Oh, I'm so sorry. And their son?"

"Oh, he's working down by the docks at the Embarcadero, just as his father did. I see him every once in a while, ma'am. He's a fine, husky young man, lots of good sense and likes his work. Well, I'd best be getting on with trimming that privet for you. It's good to have you and your aunt living here again. Not that the MacIntyres didn't appreciate my work, but, well, I've done work for this old house and the Dade family for a long time, and it does a man good in these changing times to know that he's still working for the same fine people."

"Why, thank you, Mr. Jennings. Your brother Luke made the garden very beautiful. I remember it when I was a little girl, and you're keeping it just as lovely for me. Thank you so much."

By the end of the second week in April, Aunt Clara and I were settling down to a placid routine. With Rosie Murphy on hand to prepare our meals and keep the house spic-and-span, and Henry Jennings to keep the garden thriving and to be on hand whenever we needed him for any mechanical repairs, I began to feel back home at last. My own room when I was a child had been on the second floor to the left of the landing. Its window looked out to the east, toward Coit Tower and the Bay, and on a bright day I could see the eternal gulls sweeping down from the sky to remind me once again that San Francisco is one of the world's great waterfronts. Out there where the gulls dipped and soared, the merchant fleet that my grandfather had organized and my own father had modernized began and ended its journeyings.

Aunt Clara took one of the guest rooms at the other end of the landing. There were in all some six rooms on the second floor and eight on the first, if you counted the rather spacious pantry. She had urged me to take the master bedroom, which had belonged to my parents, but I told her that I was quite content with my old room. Rosie Murphy stayed with us, and her quarters were in the small guest room on the first floor. Perhaps, since there were only the three of us in the house, I felt subconsciously that being on the second floor was more protective in the event of burglars. Perhaps it was a childish whim, but the fact was that I liked my little room with its cheerful view.

On Saturday afternoon of that second week, Aunt Clara and I decided to go downtown to do some shopping. She wanted a new dress from Magnin's, and I wanted to buy myself a new purse. The one I had was somewhat frayed, and the zipper often jammed. We went to Enrico's for lunch, and then I accompanied her to Magnin's and helped her select an attractive dark brown silk dress, which she planned to wear to her board meetings. The day had been bright, but by mid-afternoon, there was a dampness in the air and wisps of fog had begun to creep in from the Bay.

Aunt Clara's asthma had become progressively worse through the years, and many a night back at the apartment on the Avenues she had wakened me with a fit of coughing. The doctors had told her that a drier climate would be much more beneficial, but she had refused to consider the idea. San Francisco was her home, and San Francisco was where she intended to end her days, she always maintained. So when it grew damper, she excused herself and took a cab home while I meandered down along Geary Boulevard and on to Powell Street, where the cablecar begins.

Ever since we had left Magnin's, I had had the feeling that someone was following us. When I had stopped to hail a cab and then to help Aunt Clara into it, I had thought I caught out of the corner of my eye a glimpse of a little man with a cap pulled down over his face ducking back into the doorway of a little haberdashery shop. I lost sight of him for a few moments, but when I turned down Powell Street toward Market, I was conscious that he was not far behind me. Instinctively, I clutched my old purse more tightly and quickened my footsteps.

When I got to the corner of Powell and Market, I turned to look behind me. He was about fifty feet away, lighting a cigarette, and then he took a long drag at it, exhaled the smoke, and took off his cap and readjusted it, pulling it down on the other side of his face this time. I decided to cross to the other side of the street and then go back to Geary Boulevard. I remembered there'd been a small shop that displayed women's purses, gloves, and umbrellas, and very possibly I might find something suitable there. All of a sudden, I felt a tug at my purse, and the next thing I knew it had been pulled out of my grasp. I uttered a startled cry and saw the little man with the cap running back down toward Market Street. I called after him, "Stop him! He's stolen my purse!"

And then to my surprise I saw a man get out of a cab parked at the curb and run after the thief. He cornered him, grabbed him by the scruff of the neck, shook him the way a terrier shakes a rat, and retrieved my fallen purse, while a policeman hurried over from his traffic stand in the middle of Market Street to make the arrest. I saw the man who had saved my purse gesturing toward me and talking to the policeman, who promptly handcuffed the prisoner, made him back against the wall of a building, and then blew his whistle to summon aid. Meanwhile, my rescuer walked back toward me holding my purse in one hand and removing his own hat with the other, a smile on his face.

It was an extremely handsome face, too. He was six feet tall, with neatly cut black hair—and, thank heaven, none of the greasy creams or other toiletries you see prescribed for men on television so often these days! He had blue eyes and a straight nose and a firm mouth. Remembering Jim Kinsolving, I must confess that my heart quickened its beat a little when my rescuer came up to me. "Here you are, Miss," he said in a resonant baritone voice, "I hope nothing's missing. Perhaps you'd better have a look."

"I'm very grateful to you. But how in the world did you happen to notice? It all happened so quickly." I opened the purse and hastily confirmed its contents. Nothing had been taken, and the house keys (I had had a set of duplicates made for Aunt Clara so that she could come and go as she wished) and my little billfold with three hundred dollars in cash were safe and sound.

"I was going to Le Boeuf to meet a business associate of mine for a quick drink, and my cab driver was writing down his trip reports, so he hadn't started yet. I happened to be glancing in your direction, and I saw that fellow make a grab for your purse."

"Well, I'm awfully glad you did, Mr. . . . ?" I looked at him questioningly, and I felt my cheeks flush as his smile deepened. "My name's Alan Caswell. And I'm glad to have been of service. I'll have to admit something myself."

"Oh? What's that, Mr. Caswell?"

"I probably don't deserve quite so much credit for being alert, because I was really looking at you. You're the loveliest girl I've seen in San Francisco in a long, long time."

Now my cheeks were really burning. But I was also still a little flustered from the experience, and I hadn't quite registered his name. I repeated it as I stammered, "I'm sure that isn't true, Mr. Caswell. Caswell—but that name's familiar to me."

"Then I'm doubly blessed in having come to your rescue. And might I know your name?"

"It's Arlene Dade."

Alan Caswell chuckled and shook his head. "I won't give you the usual cliche about its being a small world, Miss Dade. But it happens to be true in our case, I believe. That is, if you're the Arlene Dade of Dade Navigation."

"I'm afraid I have to plead guilty on that count, Mr. Caswell."

"Then it's not strange that my name should be familiar to you, Miss Dade. My grandfather Henry Caswell and your grandfather John Dade were once partners together in that company. But that's all past history, of course. And I'm much more interested in present-day history. Because today is going to go down as the most memorable of my entire life. It's the day when I met the most beautiful girl in San Francisco."

"Please stop saying that, Mr. Caswell—you're making me frightfully embarrassed!" I could feel my blush spread to my temples and my throat, and I saw that people were staring at us. A police wagon, its siren blaring, had just stopped at the corner, and the traffic officer was jostling the little man with the cap into the back as one of the other officers opened the door. "I hope they won't be too hard on him. Maybe he was hungry and needed money for food."

"Not only beautiful, but compassionate," Alan Caswell interposed. "Don't you think I deserve a reward, Miss Dade, for my heroic action?"

The crowd of passersby was really gathering in force around us now, and I could detect that some of them were hanging on our every word. Aunt Clara would have had a conniption fit if she had seen the episode, because she would have dreaded the possible tabloid publicity certain to follow. So I thought it best that my rescuer and I leave the immediate vicinity. "Of course you do," I hastily agreed. "Would I be too forward if I asked you to take me to Le Boeuf so I can stand treat for a drink?"

He took my elbow and gallantly ushered me to the still-waiting cab. "If you hadn't offered that yourself, Miss Dade," he answered as he seated himself beside me, "I might have been tempted to kidnap you so that you could do exactly that."

And that was how I met Alan Caswell, the man who was to replace Jim Kinsolving in my life. The man who was to change my life in so many ways that I could never have even suspected in my wildest dreams.

Chapter EIGHT

THAT WAS how it all began. I suppose Aunt Clara would have thought it brazen of me to invite myself along to have a drink with a man whom I had just met and under such unusual circumstances. Perhaps that was why I did it, wanting to break loose from the restraint that had been placed over me ever since my parents' death. Perhaps, too, it was out of a spirit of pure contrariness; yes, as I went along with Alan Caswell in a cab to Le Boeuf, my mind was composed enough to remember precisely what Douglas Murray had told me about Alan Caswell's grandfather and my own. On the other hand, Alan Caswell had already told me that he and his father had had no connection with the Dade Navigation Company. And why, after all, if I found Alan Caswell himself personable and charming, as well as excitingly quick-thinking (his chase after the thief and the regaining of my purse had been done with a sophisticated flair I was quite feminine enough to admire), shouldn't I grant myself the pleasure of his company?

At any rate, we went along to the handsome

new restaurant where many of the city's elite gathered for cocktails before and after the theater and for dinner, and we had that drink. He begged my indulgence to allow him to chat with his friend for a few moments—first introducing me to him—went off to one side of the bar, and engaged in animated conversation for a few moments. Then his friend left, after coming by the table where I was sitting and courteously expressing his pleasure at having met me. Then Alan Caswell sat down opposite me and smiled. And I was lost.

His conversation that afternoon wasn't earthshaking in the least. It was witty, yes, and it was full of flowery flattery. He kept remarking how fortunate he was to have met the loveliest girl in San Francisco, and I told him to stop saying such a nonsensical and untrue thing. To this, lifting his glass to me in toast, he promptly replied, "Miss Dade, I'm quite aware that you must be aware in turn of your position in this city. And you probably think that I'm an opportunist, maybe even a fortune hunter. That's not important. What is important is that you believe me when I say what I've just said. I've the feeling that you're quite a modern and worldly young lady, no matter what your education has been. You've a spirited nature, as I can tell already by the conversation we had on Powell Street a little while ago. A blue-blooded debutante might have fainted dead away or else thrown a fit of hysteria.

You did neither. So that tells me that you're not at all naïve."

"No, I'm not naïve, Mr. Caswell," I laughed. "And that's why I find it all the more difficult to believe what you're saying. You're probably said it to at least a dozen girls since you left high school."

"Thirteen," he corrected in a calm tone of voice, and stared at me with a perfectly bland expression. Then I caught the twinkle in his eyes, and we both started to laugh. "Then, if you're not naïve," he went on, "you ought to be aware of the axiom good Doctor Freud laid down as gospel many years ago, that a woman's beauty lies in a man's desire for her. If I think you're beautiful, ergo, you're beautiful. It's really as simple as that. I don't believe in being a hypocrite, and I don't have time to waste in long courtships."

"Courtships?" I echoed. "Now there's a word that sets you down as being turn-of-the-century instead of a modernist, Mr. Caswell."

"Alan, please. And as part of my reward for saving your purse, let me call you Arlene. It's an enchanting name and well worthy of its owner."

Even though the lights at Le Boeuf were muted, I'm sure that Alan Caswell saw my blush. I had never really met anyone quite like him before. Jim Kinsolving had been direct, yes, but without any of the polish and the flowery gallantry that fairly emanated from Alan Caswell. A tiny part of my conscious mind told me that this was exactly the way a man who had my financial and social position in mind might try to befriend me. But I angrily dismissed it, because I've never believed that any two experiences can be exactly the same. Yes, I still remembered Aunt Clara and her mining engineer. But I was certain that I could see through Alan Caswell if he turned out to be like her fickle and cash-counting beau.

"You've nothing to say to that?" he pursued, beckoning to the waiter to bring us another round of drinks.

I shook my head. "I'm not vain enough to take such an exaggerated and inaccurate compliment as gospel truth, even if you do, Mr. Caswell." I pretended to be very stern with him, but he had the most irresistible grin, and once again we both burst out laughing. The waiter, setting down the drinks, eyed us with no little suspicion, possibly thinking that we might be the kind who got intoxicated on a single dry martini. "I want to see you again, Arlene," his voice was low and his gaze unwavering now.

"I'm listed in the phone book, Alan," I said, finally granting him part of his requested reward. He reached across the table, took my hand in his, and bore it to his lips. I shivered, because there was something magnetic about him. And all at once I was remembering the stolen hours with Jim Kinsolving, when the two of us had thought that we could plan for happiness of the simple and uncomplicated kind in a world where simplicity has long been considered decadent.

"Then I'll call you, and very soon."

"But won't you tell me a little about yourself first, Alan?" I entreated.

He lit a cigarette after offering me one, which I declined. "I'll make it concise as possible. I'll be twenty-eight in November, I'm a bachelor, a graduate of the University of California at Berkeley, and I hold a broker's license in the firm of Saltos, Burroughs, and Kenby, on Montgomery Street. One of the better stock and investment firms, you'll find, if you care to check."

"And your father?"

"He died five years ago, Arlene. He was a senior member of the same firm, and that's how I got in there, to be honest with you. But I rather like it, and I'm told I'm doing well and have a future. As to my financial status, I'm not exactly poor— though hardly in the same category as a certain beautiful young woman with whom I have the pleasure to be sharing a very excellent dry martini." He lifted his glass again and finished his drink.

"You didn't have to add that last, Alan," I chided him, flushing again.

I was about to add something when he leaned forward across the table and said very earnestly, "Look, Arlene, you've got two choices in life. Either, because you are who you are and what you are, you're going to build a barrier around yourself, surround yourself with servants and well-meaning relatives and friends, and live in a glass house and have private detectives shadowing your every move and wind up utterly miserable, a snob, and maybe an old maid to boot; or you're going to say to yourself that you've got brains enough and independent spirit enough to make your own decisions in life and that the money you happen to have inherited really doesn't make any difference because it was an accident. You might have been born to a poor tailor on Buchanan Street and not even have finished high school, and the fact would still remain that I find you the most desirable and lovely girl I've seen in this city since I was old enough to notice the opposite sex."

I think that speech of his, more than anything else, decided me then and there, that sunny April afternoon, to follow the dictates of my heart and to turn a deaf ear to the nagging voice of obligation and duty as well as the promptings of Aunt Clara. We parted shortly after, and I told him that I'd welcome hearing from him again whenever he wished. And then I went back home, to find that Aunt Clara was taking a hot bath and going to bed with a supper tray sent up because she had had another attack of asthma and was feeling wretched. I looked in one her and sympathized properly, and I didn't tell her anything about the theft of my purse or about Alan Caswell. There would be time enough to tell her when and if he called—when and if I saw him again.

I had never really thought much about my looks one way or another. But I have to confess that after I had left Aunt Clara, I went straight to my room, locked the door, and stared for a long time at myself in the oval-shaped, walnut-framed mirror atop my elegant chiffonier. No, I couldn't agree with him. Mother had been much lovelier, and my photographs of her taken at the time of her marriage to my father would certainly prove it. For my height of five feet six inches, I might possibly be called a trifle meager. My long legs and almost boyishly sleek hips certainly don't suggest the voluptuous sexpot of the girlie magazines, and my bosom, though well shaped and firm, is certainly not pronounced enough to draw stares in an era when topless waitresses are all the vogue.

True, my face isn't too unattrative, with my dark brown hair in a long pageboy with the curls turned upward framing its oval cast, and my slightly large blue eyes are well set apart by the bridge of a delicate Grecian nose with somewhat sensuously flaring nostrils. My mouth is certainly a trifle too large for real beauty, though I can smile without the icy pretense of other girls my age in the social whirl. Perhaps I'm proudest of all of my fine-grained creamy skin and my good health—which is much more important than artificial beauty. Jim Kinsolving had found my body exciting and rewarding, and I had welcomed his own candid virility and the unalloyed affection that he'd given me. Beautiful? No, not even if I were vain enough to allow Alan Caswell's remark to turn my head, could I in all honesty have accepted such a tribute.

And yet—and yet I kept staring at myself in that mirror for a long while until I at last blushed and laughed at my own childishness. The simple crux of the matter was that he was a debonair, worldly young bachelor with a quick mind and good reflexes. He was quite personable, and that was all. Though I didn't quite believe his remark about having said the same thing to a baker's dozen other women, I wasn't childish enough to think that he was totally inexperienced with them. Compliments came too readily to his lips, and his impeccable manners even on a cocktail date suggested many such a rendezvous.

But if it were a mild flirtation, no harm could be done. And I would welcome the diversion because of the very proper and cloistered life that I now had to lead, even after having come of age and still, for all my theoretical independence, being under the vigilant supervision of Aunt Clara.

Alan Caswell, though I could only conjecture about his amatory experience, was certainly no novice in his pursuit of me. I had made a wager with myself that he would call the very next day, but he didn't. He waited until the following Monday, while Aunt Clara and I were both having breakfast. Rosie Murphy, who had already taken enthusiastic charge of the house and, despite her youth, was behaving not unlike a mother hen with a brood of two chicks, answered the phone and then respectfully came into the little study room that Aunt Clara had decided to make over into a kind of dinette, to announce that there was a caller for me. Aunt Clara glanced at me, then asked Rosie, "Are you sure the call isn't for Miss Harwood, Rosie?"

"Oh, no, ma'am. He definitely said Miss Dade," she replied earnestly.

Aunt Clara frowned at me, and I knew that she was making a quick mental computation to discover just what men I could possibly know at this early stage. "Oh, I see," she finally drawled.

I rose from the table with studied casualness. "Thank you, Rosie," I said, and went down the hallway to the phone in the alcove.

Yes, it was Alan Caswell. He asked me to meet him for lunch. I told him it wasn't convenient, whereupon he invited me to dinner at Grison's Steak House. Unfortunately, on this particular evening, Aunt Clara didn't have one of her meetings, so I could hardly take the evening off without informing her where I was going and with whom. As I hesitated, Alan Caswell chuckled and added, "This is beginning to sound as if I were arranging a secret rendezvous with a girl from a convent. I hope it's not as bad as that, Arlene."

His jibe at my practically cloistered life decided me; I glanced back toward the dinette and then I told him, "It's nothing of the sort. Very well, I'll meet you for dinner at seven."

"Now that's the girl I met on Powell Street," he told me. "Wear something particulary revealing and come along with a good appetite. I can't stand a girl who doesn't enjoy a good meal, and Grison's is famous for big, thick, corn-fed steaks."

"I'll try not to disappoint you in your second request. I'm not sure I can take care of the first one. Just how revealingly do you want me to dress?"

"If I really told you, Arlene, we wouldn't be meeting at Grison's, but at my apartment," was the audacious answer. I couldn't help giggling. He was outrageously brash, and at least he was being direct about it. I thought about Aunt Clara's mining engineer and the cable from San Francisco; Alan Caswell didn't strike me as being that sort of scheming adventurer. Oh, there was the adventurer about him, to be sure, but he suggested a forthright, exuberant buccaneer rather than a modern confidence man.

"We were discussing my appetite for steak, Mr. Caswell," I rebuked him, "not any other kind, because it's certainly too early in our brief acquaintanceship to consider any other kind. I'll be there at seven. Thank you for inviting me." And I hung up, smiling at my own bravado.

When I went back to the dinette to finish my coffee, Aunt Clara was agog with curiosity. "Who was that, dear?" she inquired.

On the way back from the phone, I had been thinking of some plausible explanation. But Alan Caswell's directness had given me an idea; if I treated this whole matter in a secret, conspiratorial way, then Aunt Clara's suspicions would be fully aroused, and I should certainly never hear the last of it. No, the best course was honesty—at least to a point. "You remember last week when we were out shopping, Aunt Clara? Someone snatched my purse, and a very nice young man rescued it for me. I promised him that I'd have dinner with him as a kind of reward, and as a matter of fact, that was he now. I hope you won't mind if I keep the date this evening."

"Arlene! You didn't tell me that your purse was stolen! Who is this young man, anyway?"

"He happened to be in a cab nearby and saw the man grab my purse away from me, Aunt Clara. And he got out of the cab and chased the thief and turned him over to the police. He's really very nice."

"I don't dispute that in the least, Arlene, but I'd like to know his name."

I had gone too far now to turn back, unless I wanted to lie, which would have had the same effect as concealing the whole episode from the very outset. So I took a deep breath before I answered: "His name is Alan Caswell."

"Caswell? Good heavens—isn't that the name of your grandfather's former partner?" Aunt Clara gasped.

"Yes. He's Henry Caswell's grandson. He works in a very highly respected investment firm, and so did his father. He knows who I am, and that's all there is to it. It was just an accidental meeting. He did me a favor, and the least I can do is to have dinner with him and thank him properly."

"I don't like it," Aunt Clara declared, shaking her head. "Not one little bit." Then she began to cough, her face reddening and contorting from the spasm. When she had recovered, she gasped, "This wretched asthma! Why is it that some people can puff away at a carton of cigarettes a day and not have even so much as a cigarette cough, and I feel as if I were choked up with all the smoke in the world, and you know I don't even smoke!"

"You really ought to go see Doctor Hargrove, Aunt Clara," I said. "It's been much worse for you the past few months, I know."

"Humph! A lot doctors know," she sniffed. "He hasn't been able to cure me yet, and I don't think anybody ever will. It's my cross, and I just have to bear it. Though it's true, it really hadn't been too bad the last few years, just until recently. Oh, well, it'll pass, it always does. But about this Alan Caswell, dear, I still don't like the idea. There was bad blood between his grandfather and yours, and sometimes a family feud can be handed down from generation to generation."

"Good gracious, Aunt Clara!" I laughed. "You're making it sound like the Mafia! Besides, neither Alan nor his father had anything to do with the steamship company. It's all past history."

She gave me a dubious look. "I hope you're right. But I wish I'd been along, just the same."

"Now, really, Aunt Clara," I teased her, "you're perfectly capable of finding your own dates if you've a mind to. And I certainly am not going to bring you along as a duenna, for Alan would really think I was just out of a convent."

"Oh, so it's Alan already, is it?"

"Yes, it's Alan and it's Arlene. This is the year nineteen sixty-six, darling, and everybody calls everybody else by their first names. I don't go around calling you Miss Harwood, now, do I?"

"Stuff and nonsense! I'd take you across my knee if you ever did. All the same, remember that you're a Dade and that you're particularly vulnerable in all your actions so far as the newspapers are concerned."

"Yes, Aunt Clara," I responded patiently. "I'm all too well aware of my obligations. And I don't intend to shirk them, and I don't intend to disgrace the family name. And if it comforts you any, I don't propose to go to Alan's apartment right after dinner. I might even bring him here to see you."

"Now, that's the first sensible thing you've said all morning," she declared, then picked up a little silver bell and rang it for Rosie to bring her more coffee.

Chapter
NINE

I KEPT MY WORD to Aunt Clara. After a delightful dinner at Grison's Steak House, Alan Caswell drove me back in his new Impala to the house on Union Street. We had had a most enjoyable conversation, and I had found him exceptionally charming and as straightforward as in our first meeting on Powell Street and then his telephone conversation of the morning. He was impeccably groomed. wearing a pin-striped dark blue modified-double-breasted suit just coming back into the height of men's fashions and a sober tie—I couldn't help but be reminded of the hero in *The Hucksters* who had spent his last few dollars on a "sincere" tie to impress a prospective employer—and he certainly looked magnetic, successful, and very handsome as I led him into the living room to meet Aunt Clara.

She had Rosie bring us sherry from the decanter on the sideboard, and after our solicitous Irish maid had retired to her room, Aunt Clara looked Alan Caswell up and down and declared, "You're quite a man of the world, Mr. Caswell. Very elegant, not overdressed, nothing flashy. But I daresay you thought of all that before you took my niece out to dinner this evening."

Alan Caswell glanced at me with a twinkle in his eye, then nodded. "You're absolutely correct, Miss Harwood. Now, if I had been dating you, I would have had to adopt a very different campaign."

"Oh?" she was obviously intrigued. "And just what do you mean by that, young man?"

He made her a courtly bow. "You're mature, extremely sophisticated, and somewhat cynical, I have the feeling. I should have worn a suit that makes me look considerably older, and I would have taken pains to compliment you on your acumen and intellect, Miss Harwood. You would have been too much on your guard to believe anything I could have said about your considerable beauty—which I'm now privileged to behold."

"You go to the devil!" she said brusquely, but there was the hint of a smile at the corners of her lips. "Well, Arlene, I must say he's not what I expected. And he has a disarming candor. Even if he does happen to be a scoundrel—which I strongly suspect—he at least hoists his boarding flag well enough in advance for you to be forewarned."

"You're likening me to a pirate then, Miss Harwood?" Alan Caswell smiled.

"Understand me, young man, I've no wish to play the role of dragon or wicked godmother or even frantic chaperone. My niece is sensible enough and conscious enough of her position in life to take care of herself, I'm certain. But since I've brought her up after her parents' death, I can't help feeling a certain responsibility, part of which is to protect her against making any fatal errors in judgment."

"And you think I might be one of those?" he pursued.

"Quite frankly, yes." She stared at him levelly, and he met her gaze unflinchingly.

"Good," he declared at last, with an almost boyish laugh. "Then we understand each other, Miss Harwood. I met your niece quite by accident —I happened to be on hand and was privileged to do her a service—and I happen to think she's a very beautiful and desirable young woman. I can tell you in advance I have no interest in her financial status nor the social repute of her name. It only happens that I know about it, to be sure, and—"

"And by the same odd chance," Aunt Clara finished, "you happen to be the grandson of a man who had a falling-out with Arlene's grandfather. Knowing that as I do, I should naturally have my doubts about you, and you can hardly blame me."

"I don't in the least. All I can say is that my father and I have had nothing to do with the Dade Navigation Company, and I, like my father, who died a few years ago, happen to be more interested in good investments and sound stocks and bonds than in the lure of the sea, for all its profits. So with that out of the way, can we declare a truce?"

Again she gave me a wry look, and I saw grudging approval of him in that look. "I intend to investigate your background, Mr. Caswell, in the event that you plan to see a good deal more of my niece. I warn you about it in advance," she told him.

"I welcome and accept the challenge. My life is an open book. And I'll tell you franky that I plan to see a great deal of Arlene—that is, if she's willing."

"You're frank, at any rate. That's to your credit, Mr. Caswell. All right, a truce. I'll drink to it." Aunt Clara raised her glass, and Alan Caswell and I followed suit. And then for the next half hour, she began to draw him out about his schooling, his hobbies, till finally she touched on the intimate subject of his previous relationships with the opposite sex. "I told you that I'm not in the least inclined to be a meddlesome chaperone, Mr. Caswell. But since you've made it clear to me that you're going to call on Arlene and she hasn't told me that you won't be welcome, I think it only right to ask you about your outlook toward our so-called tender sex."

He chuckled, reached for a cigarette till he saw the almost imperceptible frown on Aunt Clara's face, and then replaced the pack in his coat pocket.

It was a deft little gesture that scored him a mark in her favor, as I could tell from the quick, almost smiling look she cast me. "Why, as to that, Miss Harwood, a gentleman doesn't divulge his past out of a natural inclination not to be a cad."

"Now there's a word I haven't heard used in nearly a generation," Aunt Clara responded. "And it doesn't tell me a thing. I take it you're not married, since you've already told us you're a bachelor. But how about entanglements?"

"I'd be a liar if I said I'd never looked at another girl before I met Arlene last week, Miss Harwood. Let's say only that I haven't been indiscreet or promiscuous and that I'm at the age when I want very much to find a wife who loves me and with whom I can build a happy life. My job is quite satisfactory, and it has an excellent future. If you want to know my salary without resorting to your own private means of investigation, I'll tell you right now that it's in the neighborhood of twenty thousand dollars a year. And I make a little more occasionally by playing the market, thanks to my inside information."

"You know," she said unexpectedly, "if your name were any other than Caswell, I'd almost tell Arlene that your having met her was a rather fortunate accident. I like your directness. And I see that you looked me right in the eye when you talked to me. That's a trait of breeding which appears to have been discarded lately, I'm sorry to say. And I think I've put you through enough inquisition for your first visit, Mr. Caswell. I'll take my leave of you and go to bed, and I look forward to seeing you again."

He quickly rose to his feet, seeing her prepare to rise from her armchair, and proffered his arm. She smiled at him as she accepted it. "I like your manners, too, Mr. Caswell. Good night."

I wasn't surprised when Aunt Clara made good her threat about investigating Alan Caswell's background. A week later, by which time I had had another date with him (dinner at Enrico's and then a first-rate performance of a Broadway musical at the Curran), she had Rosie summon me to her bedroom despite the lateness of the hour at which I had returned. She was already in bed, her hair in curlers, a shawl about her neck and shoulders, and Rosie had brought her a glass of hot lemonade as a lubricant against her annoying asthma.

"Well, Arlene, I have to admit that Alan Caswell has passed the preliminary test," she announced as she waved an envelope at me. I took it, opened it, and found a detailed report by a highly reputable private detective agency. Alan Caswell hadn't misrepresented himself to me. He had a responsible position at the investment company he had named, and his salary was even a few thousand dollars more than he had specified. And his father had been a member of that same firm and left him a considerable inheritance, about half of which had been the result of a spectacular coup in the market pulled off just a few months before Perry Caswell's death. Not at any time had Perry Caswell—Alan's father—attempted to find work with the Dade Navigation Company.

So much for his financial position. The report on his social life was not discouraging either. He lived in a third-floor apartment in a rather expensive and quite selective apartment hotel on Sutter Street near Divisadero. During the week, the investigator had noticed him in the company of only one other girl, an attractive auburn-haired young woman of about twenty-five who had been traced to her parents' house in San Mateo. Her name was Patricia Mallers, and her father was the vice-president of a growing electronics firm in Redwood City. The investigator had found out that Patricia Mallers had gone to the same college as Alan Caswell and that they had dated off and on for several years but that "nothing serious" was planned. This latter comment had been vouchsafed by several of the Mallers girl's neighbors.

Alan Caswell had no outstanding bills; there were no creditors breathing down his neck. The investigator had followed him to Emilio's one evening and had observed him partaking of *coq au vin*, a bottle of excellent white Burgundy, and French pastry and coffee. Three-quarters of the bottle had been imbibed, and Alan had had a glass of dry sherry as an aperitif. So there was nothing to indicate that he was a hard-drinking man in a city famous for its elbow bending. Indeed, Aunt Clara often said that there are more taverns per square block in San Francisco than in any other major metropolis of the nation, and I'd be surprised to find her inaccurate. No, there was absolutely nothing about Alan Caswell that would make him seem anything else but what he had represented himself to be—a prosperous, ambitious bachelor who had excellent taste in clothes, food, and wines, lived at an attractive address, and yet was not at all extravagant, considering his station in life.

"I hope you're satisfied, Aunt Clara." I replaced the report in the envelope and handed it back to her.

"I don't think I'll ever be satisfied with any man who comes trying to win you, Arlene. But I know that's just prejudice on my part because of my own experience. I can't hamper your life, so I leave it to you to make your own decisions. I just hope and pray that you won't do anything rash."

"Darling," I told her patiently, "let's assume that Alan Caswell was still carrying on his grandfather's mad against the Dade family. Let's even go as far as to assume that he might marry me. Now don't look so surprised, Aunt Clara. I said 'might,' though I do admit he's fun to be with and he sends tingles up and down my spine—and that's hardly a bad beginning when a girl's looking for husband material."

"You are utterly out of your mind, Arlene

Dade, if you're thinking about marriage so soon. You've just about every eligible bachelor in San Francisco to choose from, and you're still much too young. I've reconciled myself to the fact that it won't hurt you to have an occasional acceptable male escort here and there to fashionable places. The publicity might even help, if you choose wisely. And I don't object to Alan Caswell, so he may be numbered among your escorts. But you aren't honestly serious in considering him as a possible husband?"

"He hasn't asked me yet, Aunt Clara. But you didn't let me finish. As I was saying, even assuming that he hates the Dades and that he marries me, there's absolutely nothing he can do to hurt the company. I'm not exactly the silly flibberty-gibbet you might think. As a matter of fact, I called Douglas Murray yesterday afternoon and asked him just how the community-property law works in California. And do you know what he told me? That when a man marries a woman in this state, he only gets half of the holdings or money she acquires after the marriage, not before. So that means that if I did marry Alan, he still wouldn't have a thing to do with my majority stock. That should set your mind at rest."

Aunt Clara took a long sip of hot lemonade and grimaced, then coughed. She slowly shook her head. "Just on general principles, Arlene, I don't approve of marrying the first man you take a fancy to. It's no more sensible at your age now than it was back when you finished high school. You're still very young and very impressionable. I want you to get out more and not to lead such a sheltered life. And I've already told you I shan't object to Alan Caswell's taking you around where you can be seen by the right people. But that's as far as I personally think it ought to go, if you really want my advice, dear."

I had always followed Aunt Clara's advice, with that one exception of Jim Kinsolving. So I said to her, as gently as I could, "I'll always want your advice, dear Aunt Clara." But my right hand was behind my back, and my index finger and middle finger were crossed.

Chapter
TEN

ALAN CASWELL and I were married on Saturday, June 4th, at St. Mary's Cathedral, on California Avenue just at the boundary of Chinatown.

All through May, Alan and I had gone out on the town, dining and dancing, seeing the latest shows, or driving in his Impala to enjoy the scenic glories of the City by the Golden Gate and well beyond, even down to Carmel and Big Sur. It had been a month of sunshine and laughter and gaiety and love. He was comfortable to be with, easygoing, with no mercurial moods, a keen mind and a ready spirit of adventure. One evening, when we found a musical comedy at the Geary too dull, he whispered to me at intermission, "Let's drive out to the Golden Gate Bridge, park the car, and walk across. There's a full moon tonight." And we did just that.

He proposed to me two weeks before our marriage, and when I said "yes" we became lovers that very night at his apartment. It was thrilling, sweet, fiery, and rhapsodic, and Jim Kinsolving's gentleness had prepared me to understand what it could be like to be a woman and to give oneself to a man you truly loved. Yes, I'm not ashamed to say it, I was in love with Alan Caswell, body and soul. And I wasn't trying to prove anything, except that the night he proposed, I wanted him so badly that I didn't want to wait until marriage.

There was a crowd of reporters outside the church, and Aunt Clara came out behind us as matron of honor in a dress she herself had designed for the occasion. She wasn't smiling, and she hadn't approved, not even when I'd told her the very next morning after getting my proposal that I was going to become Mrs. Alan Caswell. "I guess there's no use of my saying anything, Arlene dear," she had said, "so I'm going to wish you and Alan every happiness. I only wish you hadn't been quite so hasty. You could have married him in the fall just as well, you know."

"We love each other, and we want to be together as soon as we can, Aunt Clara," I had told her happily, and I had only hoped that my secret joy in having found my love the night before wasn't shining out of my eyes so blazingly that Aunt Clara would suspect that I hadn't been exactly mid-Victorian. She didn't, because she bought me my wedding gown, of pure white organdy, and the veil and the bouquet. Poor Alan had no relatives to watch at our wedding, but I invited Douglas Murray and his senior partner, Mr. Husing, as well as Henry Pitt and William Pearson and their wives.

Douglas Murray gave me away, and I let dear old Mr. Pitt be the best man. He was a little wizened man, almost completely bald, but with incredibly bushy white eyebrows and fierce dark blue eyes. His energy and his enthusiasm were those of a man half his age, and I could understand why Douglas Murray spoke so highly of him as the company's general manager. I think my gesture in asking him to be best man pleased him a great deal, for at the end of the ceremony and after Alan and I had turned to each other and exchanged the kiss that pledged our troth for all eternity, Henry Pitt was blinking and impatiently dabbing at his eyes with a handkerchief while he grumbled something about the stuffiness of the atmosphere.

And in turn, he had a wedding present for me, one that I wouldn't have thought of, even though, of course, I had the power to order it—a honeymoon trip on the *Asturia* to Hawaii. We were to be there for the entire month of June, and the liner would dock at Honolulu on her way back from Japan to pick us up and bring us back to San Francisco just after the Fourth of July.

As we came out of the church, I was radiant with happiness, and I'd just told Alan about the honeymoon trip. We were to leave the very next day. "Darling," I whispered, squeezing his hand, "I'll tell you a little secret now. When I finished high school, Aunt Clara gave me a trip to Hawaii, and I said to myself that one day I'd go back there on my honeymoon. And I have my wish, and I'm going with the man I love. I do love you so, Alan."

"I see I've married a very sentimental creature after all," he teased me. And then, for the benefit of the photographers, he took me in his arms and gave me an even more satisfying kiss than he had before the altar.

From the church, we went to a wedding reception and supper at the lordly St. Francis, which overlooks beautiful and historic Union Square. It's in the very heart of the city, surrounded by all the gay shops, the theaters, and the bustling business district of Montgomery Street. I had never felt so much a native San Franciscan as I did when the manager of the hotel came forward in the lobby to wecome me by my new name and to lead me himself to the private dining room where the reception was to be held, adding his own personal good wishes for the happiness of our marriage.

And when Alan toasted me in champagne and, lifting his glass, said to the select guests and my very dear Aunt Clara, "To the most beautiful bride the sun ever shined on in San Francisco!" my happiness was complete. I had everything in life I wanted. Now I could begin to live a full and happy life, a useful one as the wife of the man I loved. It would be a challenging role, because there would always be between us his knowledge of my inheritance and my position as a young owner of the Dade Navigation Company. And I had sworn to myself never to let him be conscious of my greater financial worth. Because this wasn't to be a marriage for social or financial reasons; it was a marriage conceived in love and would be, I fervently prayed, nurtured in the same wonderful way.

At the end of the reception, Douglas Murray left his seat and came over to my chair, bent down to whisper to me. "My warmest congratulations, Arlene. You know that I wish you and Alan every happiness. My file clerk has just come upon some documents and a diary which belonged to your grandfather. We'd been storing that file cabinet and some other old papers in a closet that hasn't been looked into in years, you see. And ever since your twenty-first birthday, I've been wanting to track down all I could find so that you'd have the whole story of the company that belongs to you. Shall I have them sent to your stateroom in the *Asturia*?"

"They can wait till we come back from our honeymoon, Mr. Murray," I replied laughingly.

Alan, who had been chatting with Aunt Clara, turned to me and chided, "What's this? We've been married not more than an hour or so, and you're already flirting with another man."

"Not flirting, darling, just talking business. Even a loving wife is entitled to a few secrets from her husband, isn't she?" I quipped.

Alan Caswell looked at me for a moment, and I could have sworn that I saw his eyes narrow and his face grow strangely pensive. And then as suddenly as that look had come upon him it vanished and was replaced by the boyish, heartwarming smile that had the power to make me flush with mounting anticipation of the delight that the two of us could share between us.

I've often thought that diaries are something like students' examination preps; they can only suggest and jog the memory into the thousand and one exquisite little nuances of happiness. To spell out every answer and to leave no phrase unfinished would be clinical. All I remember of that heavenly month was the warmth and beauty of Hawaii and the feeling I had that nature had here created an idyllic paradise destined just for the two of us. If I had had the slightest doubts about Alan from the outset, he dispelled them with his love. He was attentive without being obsequious, gallant without being melodramatic, and always so thoroughly male. And yet what I remember most is that he considered me as a person, yet didn't hesitate to argue with me when he felt that my viewpoint was wrong. They weren't lovers' spats at all; what I mean is that I might say something about the way a special dish was prepared at one of the restaurants in Honolulu, and Alan would challenge my accuracy by pointing out something I had quite overlooked. And from then on we might go to a discussion of volcanic soil, and so on. It was mentally stimulating, and so I was never allowed to feel that he was simply deferring to me as a new husband is traditionally supposed to do in order to coddle his bride into an ethereal state of bliss. No—Alan was good for me, and I think I was good for him. And I could foresee a good life ahead for the two of us.

We had discussed the future several times during that month—when we could find the time for solemnness, which wasn't often. "I like my work, Arlene, and it's quite sufficient to give me a good living so that I could provide for you if you were King Cophetua's beggar-maid," he averred. "And I'll be frank with you, Arlene—I don't believe in ostentatious show just because a person has money. You and I could live very comfortably on my salary, and you know it. Oh, I couldn't afford a cruise like this too often, but we'd manage."

I brushed his lips with my fingertips. "Silly. As if I cared where we went or whether we stayed at home, so long as we're together."

"And I don't intend to interfere with anything you want to do with your shipping company," he continued, looking very serious and making me want to kiss him just to see that boyish grin again.

"There's really no need for me to do anything about the company, Alan. Mr. Pitt and Mr. Pearson are managing it beautifully. I'm in the happy if somewhat parasitical position of sitting back and letting them make money for me, that's all it amounts to," was my reply. "But Alan darling, if you ever feel that you'd like to take an interest in the company, just tell me. I'm sure there'd be a job for you."

"No thanks, Arlene. You know what the newspaper reporters would say if I even wanted to accept it? That I'd married you to get my hands on it because of the row your grandfather and mine once had. We'll just drop the subject, shall we, dearest?"

I even sent Aunt Clara an airmail letter telling her of that conversation, as a kind of I-told-you-so gesture to prove to her that I hadn't made a mistake about Alan Caswell. And since all good things must eventually come to an end, our month in paradise ended much too soon, and once again we were aboard the *Asturia* on our way back to San Francisco. On the last night before docking, Alan stood with me at the rail, both of us enjoying the full moon and the endless stretch of dark blue water. He slipped his left arm around my waist and murmured, "I almost wish we weren't going back, darling."

"So do I, Alan dear."

"Because I can't help thinking that when we do get back to San Francisco you'll disembark off the ship that you own, and even though you're my own wonderful, beloved wife, you're still the one everybody respects and admires."

"But surely you're not jealous of that, Alan. Wasn't it you who said that you'd make a life for us and that it didn't matter what I was?"

"That's very true. We were out there thousands

of miles away from the world into which you were trained to take your rightful place, Arlene. No, of course I'm not jealous. I'm only beginning to become aware of how very much I want to do things for you, get to the top so that people will say, 'That's Mrs. Alan Caswell,' not, 'That's the husband of Arlene Dade, the shipping heiress.' I guess I'm just remembering that in this world it's the man's place to be the successful one. Forgive me, darling. I wish this trip would never end."

"It needn't, Alan." I turned to face him, and the moon brightened our faces. "I'll always be content with what you do, so long as you always love me."

He took me by the shoulders and kissed me on the forehead. "You don't have to ask that, Arlene. You know, I was just wondering about when we get back. Would you like to leave that old house and take up your wifely housekeeping in my bachelor apartment?"

"If you'd like me to, of course I would, Alan. Though I'd hate to leave Aunt Clara in that big old house all by herself just with Rosie and once in a while Henry Jennings, the caretaker, to talk to."

"You know"—he held me closer now—"I've never really had a house of my own. You know—no, it's just a whim. . . ."

"Tell me, darling," I insisted.

"It would be wonderful living with you there in that house and pretending that it was all ours and that nobody could ever both us and that I could have you all to myself." His mouth came down on mine, and I thrilled again to the new insight I had of my precious husband. He could be so debonair and so sophisticated at times, but at moments like this he was almost like a little boy crying for the moon. And I could give it to him, that was the good part.

"Of course, Alan darling," I whispered back. "There's plenty of room for us and for Aunt Clara, too. Two whole floors. We'll take the master bedroom that my parents had, and Aunt Clara's already on the second floor and quite comfortable. And that way, we can be alone, and still I won't feel that I'm leaving Aunt Clara. Don't you see? That's a much better idea than moving to your apartment and leaving her alone in that big old house."

"And there's the practical side of it too," Alan chuckled as he kissed my eyelids and the tip of my nose in the endearing way I loved. "I could give up my place and spend the money on buying all sorts of foolish gewgaws for my girl. It's going to be fun, Arlene."

As he kissed me, his eyes looked deep into mine. The moon had shaped out its own path across the smooth dark blue water, and there were no shadows in its path as it reached us and enfolded us. But beyond its rays and beyond its benign aura, these were unsuspected shadows that I could not see as I returned my husband's kiss.

Chapter
ELEVEN

WITHIN A WEEK after I returned from Hawaii, Alan had given up his apartment and moved his belongings into the house on Union Street. During that week, he stayed at the office a good deal of the time and didn't come back until very late at night. He had work to take care of, he explained—clients of the firm to call on and commissions to undertake for them in the investment house, and other matters he had put aside during our idyllic absence from San Francisco.

Aunt Clara rather welcomed the idea of having him live with me in the house. "I will say," she grudgingly admitted over lunch the Saturday noon of our first week back, "that in spite of our most congenial neighbors, it does get lonesome here with just Rosie and myself. Especially at nighttime. Tell me, Arlene, are you happy?"

"Never more so, Aunt Clara. He's everything I've wanted a husband to be. He doesn't idolize me, and I don't want him to, and he often stands up to me and tells me when he thinks I'm wrong. I like that in him. And he's ambitious."

"Oh, that goes without saying," Aunt Clara said sarcastically. "But I should think that now his ambitions should be quieted somewhat, considering that he's brought off the prize catch of the season."

"Aunt Clara!" I reproached her. "I don't mean that at all. He's told me that he's ambitious. He wants to make good and to be respected for himself so that nobody will think of him as Arlene Dade's husband. I wouldn't think much of a man if he didn't have a sense of pride and a desire for achievement. It's quite possible that Mr. Pitt or Mr. Pearson can find a place for him in the company. But I'm not going to suggest it now."

"I shouldn't think so," Aunt Clara countered tartly. "He doesn't really have to work for a living now, you know. And if he ever decided to divorce you, I'm quite certain that he'd hold out for a sizable settlement."

"What's got into you today, Aunt Clara?" I demanded. "I thought you liked him. And I know that I love him. Isn't that enough?"

"I can't get over the suspicions of a lifetime, darling. Yes, I'll agree that he's likable and that he's behaved very decently to me. At least he didn't try to butter me up—I'd have smelled a rat if he'd tried it. But it's still much too soon for me to endorse your matrimonial choice wholeheartedly, Arlene."

"We'll let it go at that, then, Aunt Clara. And there's one good thing about our being together

—you'll be able to see for yourself just the kind of husband he is. And maybe you'll learn to appreciate him and his good qualities without always having premonitions about fortune hunters."

"Well," she retorted, "so long as you don't lose your senses completely and deed over the company to him, I daresay there's no real danger. And his superiors at that investment firm seem to think highly of him. We'll say no more about it for the present." Then she gave me a pathetic little smile, quite in contrast with her almost acidulous attitude during most of this conversation. "After all, Arlene, I want you to have the happiness that I never had. I suppose in my case, it's once bitten, twice shy. And maybe if I'd been more practical in those early days, I'd have compromised and understood that there's a price you have to pay for everything. We did get along rather famously at first." She looked away from me, toward the window, nostalgically closing her eyes for a moment. "Perhaps if he'd known that he had the security of the Harwood money, he might have forgotten his greediness and turned out to be a good husband after all. But I'll never know that now."

Touched at this rare sign of emotion from her, I put my hand over hers and whispered, "Maybe I shouldn't let him stay here with us, then, Aunt Clara. I feel as if the two of us were flaunting our happiness in your face, and I don't want to do that to you."

She reached for her handkerchief and irritatedly blew her nose. Once again she was her practical, somewhat cynical self. "Now don't go maudlin on me, Arlene, for pity's sake! And stop trying to make out as if I begrudge your happiness, yours and that handsome husband's. No such thing! I guess I can be allowed to feel sorry for myself just once when my niece gets married, can't I?" And she blew her nose again and gave me a scathing look that made me laugh, knowing that we had come to an amicable accord.

"You have your privacy, just as always, Aunt Clara. We'll be on the first floor, and you'll be on the second," I assured her. "How's your asthma been behaving while we were away?"

"Well, fortunately, we've had sunshine and passably warm evenings," she admitted, "It hasn't been too bad this past month. Oh, you almost made me forget!"

"Forget?"

She nodded. "A few days after you and Alan left on the *Asturia,* Mr. Murray sent a package from his office over to you by messenger. There was a note saying that you'd want to look at it when you got back. I kept it in my room, but I guess in all the excitement of your returning and the plans for having Alan move in here, I quite forgot it."

"I'll have Rosie fetch it, dear. Just you relax and have a little more iced tea." I reached for the little silver bell, and Rosie promptly appeared, with a smiling greeting.

Aunt Clara chuckled as she eyed the maid. "I'm inclined to think you're becoming Rosie's special favorite, Arlene. But maybe it's the glamor of a trip to Hawaii. Rosie was saying, while you were gone, that she'd always wanted to go there."

"I hope someday you will, Rosie. And you can go on one of our ships, too," I promised. Then, to Aunt Clara: "Where shall she look for the package, Aunt Clara?"

"Rosie, there's a parcel wrapped in brown paper in my bottom bureau drawer, under my cashmere shawl. Would you bring it down and give it to Miss Arlene?"

In a few moments Rosie was back and, with an enthusiastic but gauche attempt at a curtsy, set the parcel down beside my plate, then tactfully withdrew. I unwrapped it while Aunt Clara tried her best not to show her impatient curiosity. I found a leather-bound ledger book, about the size that accountants use; a dozen or more letters in handsomely engraved envelopes whose paper was brittle and brown with age, and an old book entitled *Chambliss' Diary or Society as It Really Is,* whose spine was broken and whose blue cloth covers were bent and waterlogged.

"Good heavens!" Aunt Clara exclaimed, "What in the world is all that?" The ledger had a rotting band around it, but the catch had long since been broken, and the band sprawled limply over the scuffed leather cover.

Wonderingly, I opened its pages at random,

and I at once perceived line upon line of small crabbed handwriting in faded blue ink. Glancing at it more closely, I saw a date at the top of the right-hand page, January 17, 1906, and with some effort I was able to read a few words aloud to Aunt Clara. " 'A foggy, chilly day, with the wind blowing in off the Embarcadero. On a day like this, I'm glad our ships aren't sailing round the Cape of Good Hope. But of late there are more storms here at home than on the seven seas. Henry is either becoming senile or has always been a disgruntled, sour man. He thinks I've cheated him, but the truth is he himself was to blame for all his follies.'

"It's a diary, Aunt Clara." I thumbed through the pages back to the beginning of the ledger, and I saw the date May 26, 1894. "It covers over ten years. What a fascinating picture of San Francisco it must contain!"

"And that book, Arlene, what is it?" Aunt Clara asked.

I carefully opened the book to its title page. "It's by William H. Chambliss," I said. "The title says it's a diary too."

Aunt Clara gave a sardonic little laugh. "Vastly different from your grandfather's, you can be sure, Arlene. I remember reading about that book years ago in a newspaper supplement. It was printed in New York around eighteen ninety-five, and as soon as copies reached here, a great many prominent citizens spent a lot of time and money buying and burning every copy they could get their hands on. Mr. Chambliss didn't have much use for the cream of San Francisco society."

I had already begun to scan the book, searching for some of this invective, and I suddenly came across it in one of the early chapters. "This is really strong, Aunt Clara," I laughed. "Listen to this. 'A certain Edward Greenway, whose business is boosting the sales of a certain brand of champagne which is drunk in houses of ill fame, has taken upon himself to assemble a list of the four hundred finest families in San Francisco. He believes himself to be another Ward McAllister, but he is grossly in error. His four hundred are mostly members of the parvenucracy.'" I looked up at her. "That *is* rather strong, isn't it?"

"Go on a bit, dear," she bade me.

"All right; here's more. 'You will find in the composition of the parvenucracy such ingredients as unnatural depravity, arrogance, presumption, gross dishonesty, unpardonable ignorance, female boldness, hellish hypocrisy, and female skeletons in flimsy boxes, the limbs of which their owners essay to hold down with sacks of ill-gotten gain.'" I shook my head. "I'm amazed he wasn't sued for libel or publicly horsewhipped."

"No doubt he was, though of course, I don't recall. But I remember reading in the newspaper story what a furor that scandalous book caused when the first copies arrived in San Francisco. Of course, it was an age of double standards, none

126

for the women and two for the men. And the Barbary Coast was in full swing then. Let's see—that book came out in eighteen ninety-five. That was about the time of the great Fair scandal. I don't mean a world's fair, dear. There was a Comstock Lode millionaire and United States Senator James G. Fair, one of whose two sons married a lady of ill repute and was cut off in his father's will with a hundred dollars. Then, as I remember the story, the son and his bride were killed while driving a new Mercedes on the road to Paris, and there was a big fight over the millions left in the son's estate as well as in Senator Fair's." She sighed. "Yes, Arlene, that was a most colorful period in our history, just before the great earthquake."

As she had been speaking, I had turned back to the old diary-ledger and was idly flipping its pages, when suddenly I came upon a page, toward the end of the book, that was entirely blank except for a centered square drawn heavily in green ink. Inside the square were tiny little dots and dashes, some arranged vertically, some horizontally, and others in diagonal rows. I turned the ledger so that it faced Aunt Clara on the opposite side of the table and exclaimed, "Isn't this curious, Aunt Clara? I wonder what it is."

She took a pair of reading glasses out of their case, which she always carried in a little hand-woven cosmetic bag, ajusted them, and stared at the place I had marked with my finger. "That *is* odd," she admitted, "I'm sure I haven't the slightest idea. Your grandfather, by all I've heard about him and all I know myself, wasn't the type to doodle. Maybe it's a code of some kind, or a cipher."

She had said that casually, without thinking, and yet at that very moment a strange presentiment ran through me. I determined to read my grandfather's diary-ledger as soon as I could, and when I was alone. Perhaps it would tell me more about him. Perhaps it would cast a light on the dark mystery surrounding his dealings with his partner, Henry Caswell, the grandfather of my own husband.

Chapter
TWELVE

THE EVENING of the day that Aunt Clara had turned over to me my grandfather's letters and the unusual diary and Chambliss's vituperative book, Alan and Aunt Clara and I went out to dinner at the Cho-Cho Japanese Restaurant at the end of Kearny Street to feast on sukiyaki and yakitori (a kind of Japanese shishkebab composed of pieces of lean rib beef, chicken, giant shrimps, and mushrooms skewered on a long stick and roasted on a charcoal fire, then dipped into an enchanting sauce). Alan himself invited Aunt Clara, which I thought was very gracious of him. He had been particularly cordial to her ever since that all-important introduction; and after we had returned home and were alone in that magnificent bedroom with its four-postered canopied bed that my parents had occupied before me, I told him how very much I appreciated his doing his best to please her.

"I like her very much, Arlene dear," he told me as he lit a cigarette and glanced at himself in the elegant mirror that topped the massive and ornately scrolled set of dresser drawers directly opposite the bed. "She deals straight from the shoulder, and that's the way I like my women."

Involuntarily, I frowned; that last phrase of his had been just a bit too quick and too glib. It suggested past amours of which I knew nothing and of which I was, all of a sudden, irrationally jealous. I came toward him and put my arms around him from behind, nuzzling my chin against his shoulder. "Your women," I said reproachfully. "Do you know, you've never told me anything about that part of your life."

I could see him smile in the mirror, and he was always so magnetic and so virile when he smiled. He took a puff at his cigarette and then drawled, "I've already had my say on the subject, darling. No gentleman discusses another woman in the presence of the one he's with, especially if they're married. Besides, marriage put an end to my bachelor days. Just as I'm sure it put an end to your little flirtations—and I shan't ever ask you about them or whether you've even had them."

I was mollified by this, because I had no intion of telling him about Jim Kinsolving. And the private investigator's report had, I told myself, indicated that Alan Caswell had led an exemplary life at the time he was wooing me.

He turned now, took hold of my shoulders, and kissed me on the throat. "We'll get along just fine, you and I," he murmured. "Do you know, now that I've moved in here, I seem to have acquired the tradition, as if I'd descended from one of San Francisco's oldest and finest families. It's this beautiful furniture, this air of elegance and aristocracy everywhere. Once you come inside the door of this house, you're in a world that's past with the earthquake that leveled the city. Yet that life still goes on today."

"I feel that too, darling," I said thoughtfully, then returned his kiss. Exultantly I thought, as he picked me up in his arms and carried me off to that huge, luxurious bed, that no bride could be happier with the knowledge that her husband loved her and desired her. That was what I had wanted, and Alan Caswell had not disappointed me in any respect.

But the next day, when Aunt Clara decided to visit friends in Sausalito and Alan apologetically asked me if I'd mind if he went over to the airport to meet a friend with whom he'd gone to college and who was coming in from New York, I had my chance to read the letters and to devote my time to that thick old diary-ledger. The writing, as I've indicated, was small and angular, and I could almost visualize my grandfather sitting at the cherrywood desk in the study, bending over that book by candlelight or a kerosene lamp, perhaps near-sightedly bowing his face down toward the page as his fingers clenched a quill pen and scrawled letters on the then-white sheet. The ink had faded long ago, though some parts seemed clearer than others, and almost as if they had been written in a different hand. Yet there were unmistakable signs that the writing throughout belonged to the same man—the bold, dashing *l*'s, the tiny *e*'s that looked almost like *c*'s, and the jagged vertical stroke of the *p*'s and *q*'s.

The letters were not of great importance; mostly, they were to business associates suggesting that Dade ships be used for their cargo and quoting prices for longer hauls that were meant to best competition. There was one from a vintner in Napa Valley trying to bargain with my grandfather to lower his rates on a shipment of barrels of white wine to be sent to Baja California. But it was the diary-ledger that fascinated me the most, particularly that curious page with its boxed-off center and all the little dots and squiggles inside it. I decided to take my grandfather's diary-ledger to the attic, which not even Rosie Murphy bothered to look after. It would be a safe retreat there, and I could pretend that I was a child again, and reading what my grandfather had to say of the exciting and colorful life of the era before the great earthquake, I could almost pretend that I was part of it.

I had seen photographs of my grandfather, and I judged him to have been a vigorous, hard-bitten, and straightforward kind of man. He had a strong, rugged chin, prominent Roman nose, and closely set, piercing eyes—or so at least the old photograph showed. His high forehead denoted intellect, and he wore the sideburns and chin whiskers that were popular in that period. His mouth was firm and incisive; it was the mouth of a man who wasn't afraid of his own opinions and who would abide by them. Even without having seen that picture and made my own characterization of him through it, I could have judged what manner of man he was by his letters and by his writing in the diary-ledger.

I spent over an hour lost and absorbed in my grandfather's vivid commentaries on the San Francisco that predated the great earthquake of 1906. At times, he was inclined to be cynical about the feverish pursuit of ephemeral pleasures that his associates sought. For there were many fleshpots of those days, the parlorhouses and the gambling houses of the Barbary Coast, and all the notorious women whose own stories could form the basis of many a novel, and sometimes did. He wasn't a puritan or a moralist, but he preferred marriage to profligacy, as was evidenced by the terse phrases I encountered every so often in those faded pages. He felt himself alone, without aid from anyone in his task of pioneering a growing company into an institution that would serve the entire state and grow prosperous and make the people of San Francisco share in that prosperity.

A few pages before the curious cipher—so, at last, I had decided it must be—I came across a reference I thought might have some connection with it. It referred to the sinking of a vessel known as the *Afrikander* just off the Monterey Coast.

John Dade believed that it had had a cargo of gold and jewels belonging to a wealthy Spanish grandee who had fled the Old World, made his way to Mexico, and finally decided to move to San Francisco, where his wealth might make him one of the elite. He had embarked at one of the little ports in Baja California with an entourage comprised of a handsome young male secretary, his niece and her duenna, and a twelve-year-old male cousin. John Dade wrote that it was feared that there were no survivors and that the ship had foundered on a reef several hundred yards offshore, having been driven there by an unexpected and violent storm.

At the bottom of the next page, a reference to the ill-fated *Afrikander* appeared again in the single sentence that began a paragraph. "Salvage operations are possible, and I mean to look into it, because part of the ship still emerges above the water." Thereafter, the ink seemed to be more faded than ever, and I could hardly make out the words; yet just a page before I came again to that curious box and its unknown code, I encountered these significant words. "I have had success with my salvage venture. The valuables were recovered, but I propose to keep them as a fund for the emergencies of my descendants, if the Dade Navigation Company should ever pass away from the Dade family. It could happen, because I am not yet married and have no prospect of a son and heir. I will think about it and where I shall let it rest for safekeeping."

And then, two paragraphs later, this even more significant comment.

Henry Caswell has heard of the *Afrikander*. One of our dock hands, whom he bribes to give him gossip and rumors of all that goes on in our company as well as among our competitors, must have told him. We had dinner this evening, and he dared accuse me of having pirated the treasure he knew to be aboard that ship. He said that it belonged to the company and that he, as my partner, had an equal right. I told him he was in error. He would have been right if I had used one of the Dade vessels to accomplish the transfer or any of the Dade employees to do the diving. But I did this for myself, solely, using my own money and not that of the company; and I did it to guarantee that no matter what may happen to my fortune, I will have the wherewithal someday to take unto myself a wife and to have the child I so desire to carry on my name. I have done well by Henry Caswell, and I do not much care that he says that I have taken the bread from his very mouth. He has done it himself with his foolish speculations and his lust for fancy women and fine wines and gambling. He will not have it now or ever, and I am no thief.

I closed the book, my heart beating rapidly, and I rose and went to the gable window to look down on the narrow sidewalk. My husband was just getting out of his car. He glanced up toward the top of the house, and out of impulse—inexplicable yet powerful—I hurriedly stepped to one side so that he could not see me. I looked around me in that almost barren attic, seeking a hiding place for the diary-ledger, which I felt sure now, contained a secret from the past whose unraveling would explain mysteries that I had never known. And I saw at last an old steamer trunk, its lid slightly ajar and its old heavy brass lock broken. It would be the perfect hiding place, I thought. Carefully I lifted the top; the hinges still held fast, and I lifted the first drawer, and then the bottom one. I dropped the leather-bound book below, then let the drawers slip back as they had been. I closed the lid, leaving it slightly ajar as before, and moved the lock till it seemed to be exactly in its original position. Then I tiptoed out of the attic, closing the door as quietly as I could. Alan was on the first floor, calling to Rosie to inquire where I was. I hurried down to Aunt Clara's room, opened the door, then loudly closed it and called, "Is that you, Alan dear?"

As I went down to meet him and embrace him, I had the fleeting thought that for the first time in my married life I was guilty of guile and deception. How little I knew of those traits!

Chapter
THIRTEEN

How LONG did it take Adam and Eve to be turned out of their Garden of Eden? For Alan and myself, it took little more than two weeks.

He seemed engrossed when he returned from the airport that Sunday afternoon. His kiss, when I came down to meet him, was perfunctory, not at all the passionate and devoted embrace of the husband for whom the honeymoon should certainly not be over so soon. Aunt Clara came home about five, and Rosie prepared a collation for us of her own very tasty chicken salad, rye toast, iced tea, and a blancmange dessert. We ate in the dinette, because it seemed much too formal to seat just the three of us at that huge table in the dining room, especially on a bright summer afternoon when there was no need for ceremony. Alan devoted his attention to his food, with only an occasional remark to the two of us. I asked him brightly if he and his former college chum had had a pleasant reunion, and he only nodded. Aunt Clara glanced at him, then back at me with a wondering expressin. When he had finished, he asked to be excused, saying that he had to meet a client early Monday morning and drive him out to San Jose to look at some property whose mortgage the client was considering purchasing. I didn't pretend to know too much about investment companies, but my notion was that they dealt mainly in stocks and bonds and that mortgages were primarily a real estate transaction, so I innocently commented, "I didn't know your company handled real properties, Alan dear."

He looked over at me with what was unmistakably a scowl, then lit a cigarette and finally declared, "You never really bothered to find out what my job is, Arlene. For your information, our firm is wide-awake and not without a certain amount of speculative imagination. We occasionally handle mortgages on property that we think shows good promise. Now if you'll excuse me, Aunt Clara, Arlene, I'll take a shower, smoke a cigar, and then go early to bed. Good night."

After he had left us, Aunt Clara turned to me and asked, "What was that all about, dear? A rift in the lute so soon?"

"Of course not. Alan's tired. He's been working quite hard at the office, as you know, and he went to the airport to meet someone he knew in college."

"I see. He does seem to have something on his mind. And I rather thought he snapped your head off when you asked him about his appointment tomorrow." She took another sip of her iced tea.

"I told you what he said to me on shipboard that last night," I said with a reassuring smile. "He wouldn't be human if he didn't try to get ahead, to prove that he has merit on his own and doesn't need the name of Dade. I'm certain by now he's not a fortune hunter."

"So long as you don't sign over all your stock to him, Arlene, or make him a gift of your trust fund, I'll keep my mouth shut," Aunt Clara said with a sardonic little smile. "There's just one thing, though."

"What's that?"

She looked at me a long moment before replying, then uttered a particularly mournful sigh. "It's probably nothing, really, Arlene."

"But what is it, Aunt Clara? If you've anything on your mind, please come out with it. You know I like things direct. You know that's why I like Alan, because he's that way. And you've never hidden anything from me—please don't start now."

"All right. I was only wondering whether his former college chum happend to be male or female. Because you didn't notice while he was eating the chicken salad, but he wiped his mouth with a napkin and put it back down on his lap. And there was a spot of what looked very suspiciously like lipstick. Not at all your shade, either."

"Oh, good heavens, Aunt Clara, is that all? What if it actually was a girl instead of a fellow? What's a friendly kiss between old schoolmates?

I wouldn't expect Alan to be jealous if I kissed somebody I'd known at San Francisco State College."

"No, I know you wouldn't, dear. Only there's something else. Rosie told me Friday afternoon, after she'd sent out laundry, that she'd collected his hamper, sorted it out, and written it down to give the laundryman the list. And there was one of his handkerchiefs that smelled of a woman's perfume, and it had lipstick on it too. And it certainly wasn't your perfume. Rosie said it reeked to high heaven—to quote her verbatim, I might add."

I shrugged. "That's just circumstantial evidence, Aunt Clara. You've already set a private investigator on him and found out that apparently he doesn't have a mistress on the side. And besides, a woman can always tell when her husband is paying attention to another woman. I can assure you that Alan has been in every sense the husband I've always wanted. Please let it go at that."

"Very well—it's your life, darling. I'm not going to be a prophetess of gloom, believe me. I just can't help my own suspicious nature where men are concerned, and I don't think Rosie can either. Well, since Alan isn't going to keep us company any more this evening, let's you and I have a game of cribbage."

But from that very afternoon (a Sunday), strange, mystifying things began to happen. I staunchly refused to let Aunt Clara's bit of circumstantial accusation mar the perfect harmony Alan and I had found. I decided that it was time that I do something more than lounge about the house and go shopping and be a parasitical though happy bride, so the following Tuesday morning I called a cab and went down to the old Ferry Building and took the elevator to the tenth floor, which was entirely occupied by our office.

A pleasant middle-aged receptionist greeted me effusively once I had given her my name, and ceremoniously ushered me into the luxurious private office of William Pearson. He was a stout, genial man in his late fifties, nearly bald but with a heavy walrus mustache, and his booming voice indicated that he had still ample vitality to fill the role of sales manager of our company. I remembered his wife from the wedding reception—a charming, Dresden-doll creature, in her late forties, elegantly dressed and jeweled and very retiring, quite the antithesis of her husband. And I had observed that for all his ebullience and gusto, when he went back to her to see that she had more champagne or some of the excellent canapés the St. Francis chef had prepared for the occasion, he was unusually tender and solicitous. There could be no doubt that opposites attract in marriage; Alan and I were certainly at opposite poles in many ways. And yet in these few short months since he had first so unexpectedly met me, I had come to love him and to trust him even more than I had believed I could do with Jim Kinsolving.

In William Pearson's office were beautifully carved models of the leaders of our modern fleet, such as the *Asturia* and the *Golden Gate*. Mr. Pearson asked how he could help me, and I told him that I thought it was high time I acquainted myself with the operation of a company whose principal stockholder I was. "I haven't the least intention of snooping or prying, Mr. Pearson," I assured him, "but I want to know more about the firm which my grandfather so ably developed and to which my father gave most of his life."

"That's a tall order, Miss Dade," he chuckled, then caught himself. "Oh, I beg your pardon— Mrs. Caswell. I guess I've always been used to having a Dade around here, you know. Well, is it history you want to begin with, and then perhaps a look at the three-dimensional map in the conference room which shows where all of our ships are at this very moment?"

I nodded. "That, of course. And I'd appreciate it if you'd tell me if there are any current ventures in which the Dade Navigation Company is involved having to do with expansion of cargo or passenger routes. I'm an utter novice, and I've become very sadly aware of it. I just don't want to sit at home and clip coupons, as Aunt Clara says."

He threw back his head and laughed exuberantly, and I smiled at him, because he was such a jovial, natural, and unassuming person. Just by chatting with him all that morning—he took me to lunch at the little café near the building which served wonderful seafood—and most of that afternoon, I began to understand something of the appeal this business must have had for my grandfather and my father alike. It was a business of service; yet it was never devoid of adventure and peril. The early fishing and travel schooners had had their share of shipwrecks, being blown off course, even of occasional mutinies. The first steamships had carried more cargo than passengers, and it had taken several years to come abreast of the progress the Matson Line, our most powerful competitor, had been making at the turn of the century. Mr. Pearson was patient with me, as if I were a pupil in grammar school; yet he did not talk down to me or, on the other hand, try to browbeat me with his expert knowledge. He showed me the figures for the past several years, pointed out what part of our earnings went to expenditures for drydocking, rehabilitation of engines and furnishings, top wages with incentive bonuses for our seamen.

The old open-faced clock at the top of the Ferry Building showed four-fifteen when I finally took my leave of him and thanked him for all the time he had given me. I told him that I wanted to visit every so often and that whenever there was an important conference meeting having to do with future plans, I should very much appreciate his inviting me to sit in. "I promise I won't do anything drastic or interfere at all, because I'm still only a woman, Mr. Pearson," I told him smilingly.

"But I want to feel that I'm part of this company, and maybe even a woman can contribute an idea that will help it progress. Then maybe you can still feel that you have a Dade around here. Good afternoon, and thank you again."

I had wanted to see Henry Pitt, but the receptionist had told me that he had gone out early this morning and was not expected back for the rest of the day. As I went down in the elevator, my brain was swarming with facts and figures, with recollections of the shipwrecks and the storms and the mutinies that Mr. Pearson had so thoroughly documented to me. It had been an exhausting but certainly stimulating day. I reached the lobby, paused to buy a pack of cigarettes, and then walked out through the swinging doors, thinking all of a sudden that I might just decide to go to one of the fine restaurants I'd read about but hadn't visited yet, such as Original Joe's or Sorrento's.

I lit a cigarette and looked about. The sky was darkening, and over to the northwest, I thought I could see the first haze of the evening fog. A cab drove up to the doorway and discharged its passengers, and I got in. For a moment I hesitated, and then I told the driver to take me to Sorrento's. I felt in the mood for good Italian minestrone and veal scallopine and perhaps some spumoni for dessert. The driver tipped his cap and started up the motor. Just as we pulled away, I glanced behind me, why, I don't know. And through the rear window of my cab, I could see a white Impala pulling up to the doorway to the Ferry Building. It opened, and Henry Pitt got out and shook hands with the driver. My cab was gathering speed, so I could not identify the latter. But I would have sworn it was my husband.

Chapter FOURTEEN

BY THE MIDDLE of August, Alan Caswell and I had had our first quarrel, and I had sat in on my first board meeting of the Dade Navigation Company.

Alan hadn't been at home when I returned from my visit with Mr. Pearson, and Rosie, whom I had phoned to tell that I was staying in town for dinner, had informed me that he too had called to tell her that he would be dining with a client over in Marin County. Aunt Clara and I played cribbage until nearly ten o'clock that night, and we were just about ready to call a halt to our game when Alan came in, hung up his hat and coat on the floridly ornamental rack in the front hallway, and came into the living room.

He looked tired and drawn, and there was a scowl on his handsome face. I left the cribbage table and went to him and kissed him. It seemed to me that he returned my kiss rather absently, as if he had his mind on something else. "You've really been on the go, darling," I tried to cheer him. "But you'll see, you'll be the head of the

146

firm before very long if you keep it up. Can I get you a drink, perhaps? You must be exhausted, going to San Jose in the morning and then way over to Marin County this afternoon."

To my surprise, he glared at me, hands on hips. "Are you starting to keep a daily tab on my activities, Arlene?"

"Of course not, darling. But you said yourself you were going over to San Jose with a client today, and you phoned Rosie to say that you were taking someone to dinner in Marin County. It doesn't take any great powers of deduction to figure out how much driving you must have done. Let me get you that drink, won't you?"

"No, thanks. I think I'll go to bed, if you don't mind. How are you, Aunt Clara?"

"Apart from my asthma and a natural desire not to see my niece given a lecture so early in her marriage, I'm fine, thank you," Aunt Clara snapped.

"Well, I might have expected it," he said with a sarcastic drawl. "Two women and a maid against one mere man. The odds will always be stacked against me, so I won't argue with any of you." And off he went.

Aunt Clara collected the cards, shuffled them, and put them back into the little box. Neither of us said anything. I felt hurt, left out. And to rebuke me in front of Aunt Clara was, I thought, hardly the considerate way to do it. Alan could have waited until we were in the privacy of our bedroom. But the odd thing was that we hadn't had much of that privacy, not since that Sunday when he'd gone to the airport. There had been more nights than I cared to remember when we'd lain side by side in that huge bed while I listened to the even breathing that told me he was fast asleep. And for my part, I had no intention of pursuing him. No more than a husband should force himself on his wife simply because they happen to be married, should a wife always expect romance and passion, I had told myself.

And yet the change in his feelings toward me was so markedly different that I could not help wondering what was going wrong. Was I less desirable to him, perhaps? Had he tired of me already? Had the novelty of being married to Arlene Dade, the shipping heiress, worn off so soon? I had no standards of comparison except, of course, that brief interlude with Jim Kinsolving. Yet at the beginning of our marriage, our honeymoon had been rhapsodic, perfect, fluently communicative and ardent. Besides, Alan was young and vital, and though I no longer wanted to remember what he had first said to me about my being beautiful, I was not entirely without attractiveness for a man—not for a man who loved me, at any rate, as I thought Alan did.

As I fell asleep that night beside him, I could not help remembering the white Impala and the sight of Henry Pitt getting out and shaking hands with the driver. But what could Alan be doing with Henry Pitt, our general manager? Was it possible they had gone to Marin County together? And if they had, what common denominator could possibly have brought them together? The only time they had met, to the best of my knowledge, was at the wedding reception. I tried to dismiss this morbid and useless reasoning, and I turned toward Alan, hoping that suddenly he would take me in his arms and banish all those worrisome thoughts of mine. But he lay on his side, his back turned to me, fast asleep. With a heavy heart, I turned to my side of the bed, closed my eyes, and resolutely strove for sleep.

The board meeting was held ten days later. Mr. Pitt and Mr. Pearson sat on either side of me at the head of the table in the conference room, with that great framed map at the opposite wall. I could see tiny steamships and cargo ships with little flags fixed on the blue of the ocean and near their ports of call. It was impressive, and it was a reminder that my grandfather and my father had sat in this same chair and made that map into the scope and breadth it had today through enterprise and imagination.

George Wallace, the advertising manager, an energetic, brown-haired, eager-eyed, and newly married man in his mid-thirties, and elderly, bluff Matthew Hartigan, the company's maintenance manager, were present also, as were Philip Mattheson, our passenger-ticket sales manager, and Adam Wales, who was in charge of contracts for commercial cargo. I could see from the expressions of most of the men, with the exception of Mr. Pearson, that I was looked upon as an interloper—oh, to be sure, a delightful diversion from their serious routine of business and, judging from their occasionally admiring and deferential glances, a female power behind the throne who, though she might have not the slightest idea of what was going on, was nonetheless pleasant to look upon.

Henry Pitt, as general manager, formally opened the meeting by introducing me to those executives whom I had not yet met; then he asked for a report from each of the various department heads. I sat and listened without a word, while I heard financial statements and propoals to shorten or lengthen the route of this or that cargo or passenger ship, until finally Mr. Pearson brought before the meeting the proposal of a small independent cargo shipper near San Pedro whose owner was desirous of selling out or of merging and who had already approached him.

There was much pro-and-con discussion of this idea, and finally Mr. Pearson turned to me and asked, "Might we hear your opinion on the matter, Mrs. Caswell?"

"Thank you for including me in your discussion, Mr. Pearson." I smiled at this likable, exuberant man. "Do we gain any advantages by buying him out?"

150

"The advantages outweigh the disadvantages," he replied at once. "He owns a dozen excellent freighters, most of them in very serviceable condition. He runs from Baja California to San Diego and San Pedro, and occasionally two or three of his ships drop anchor here. The last few years, he's diverted a little of our normal hauling by cutting prices. That's run-of-the-mill competition, to be sure. But he's getting old and would like to sell out. His feeling is that he's worked hard to build his company and would like to see it continued in good hands."

"Then I think it would be a good idea to weigh his offer," I answered, "Unless, of course, you gentlemen feel that our own ships are adequate to service the area in which he's doing business."

"There's some duplication, to be sure, Mrs. Caswell," Mr. Pearson replied, "but his asking price is within reason, and I think I can get him to cut it a bit for fast action. In my opinion, we're going to be handling more and more cargo in the years ahead. I'd rather stress that than passenger service."

"I don't agree at all, Pearson," Henry Pitt intervened, his face cold and authoritative. "Take Hawaii alone. Are you aware of how many tourists the Matson people take to the islands over a year's haul? It's practically doubled in the last few years, and it's going to get bigger than ever. They're building so many luxury hotels on Waikiki Beach that there'll be hardly a square foot of sand left for the sunbather before they're done. No, I'm of the opinion we ought to pass up more cargo ships and try to expand our passenger service to Hawaii and Australia and the Orient. That's where the big money lies."

"I think we could reconcile both ideas, gentlemen," I spoke up, and everyone turned to look at me with some surprise. "You know, I've read in the travel sections of the newspapers how many schoolteachers and stenographers want to go abroad, but they haven't the money for the luxury liners. So they read the schedules of the freighters, and they go along as passengers. Its one class on a freighter, unless I'm mistaken, and it's a very enjoyable way to travel, I'm told. Why couldn't we turn some of those cargo ships Mr. Pearson wants to buy into traveling freighters that take a quota of passengers?"

"That's a capital idea, Mrs. Caswell," Adam Wales said enthusiastically, making notes on a scratch pad before him. "The only trouble is, we'd have to spend some money outfitting those ships. They're not exactly built for cruises, you know."

"Just the same, I think Mrs. Caswell has given us an excellent thought, gentlemen," William Pearson said, taking control again. I saw Henry Pitt shrug and look down at the scratch pad before him on which he had been busily writing. "I'll talk with MacMasters next week, and I'll take our capable maintenance manager along to see him in San Pedro. We'll have a looksee as to how much it really would cost to carry out Mrs. Caswell's idea. Well, gentlemen, so far as I'm concerned, that just about completes our business for today, unless you've something in mind, Henry?"

Henry Pitt looked up, and I could see that he had what looked almost like a sneer on his face. "No, Bill, you've taken the helm this voyage. I'll let you drop anchor and order up the refreshments." Then he turned to me with a sudden, effusive smile. "We'd all be delighted, Mrs. Caswell, if you'd stay and share our sailors' grog and biscuits and cheese. It's a kind of tradition after every board meeting. Old John Dade started it himself."

I willingly acquiesced, and Henry Pitt pressed a buzzer on the side of the table, and the pleasant middle-aged receptionist, Miss Gurthy, entered and was given the order to have the refreshments brought in. A few moments later, two office girls carried in trays on which were huge copper mugs filled with rum and plates of hardtack biscuits and what Aunt Clara used to call "mousetrap cheese." William Pearson lifted his mug and toasted me, and I blushingly acknowledged the toast and wished his new venture success. All eyes were on me as I attacked my ration of grog, and I felt a secret satisfaction in being able to finish nearly all of it by the time the meeting broke up.

I went home with a glow of triumph, feeling for the first time that I had fulfilled the obligations of my family name and my inheritance. Even if my little suggestion proved to be impractical, I had at least contributed something, and I felt that I wasn't quite the decorative parasite I'd been up to now.

But my joy was quickly ended when, as I stepped into the hallway of the old house on Union Street, Rosie Murphy hurried up to me and in a hushed voice told me that Aunt Clara had had a very bad attack of asthma and that Dr. Hargrove was upstairs in her room now. "She's not good at all, Mrs. Caswell," the Irish maid said, dolefully shaking her head. "Doctor Hargrove says her heart is strained, and she's got to be very quiet and very careful. And he gave me orders about her diet too. She isn't going to like them, I can tell you."

A few moments later, on the landing outside Aunt Clara's room, Dr. Floyd Hargrove, a portly, bespectacled, gray-haired man whose curt manner belied his real concern for his patients—though I had had many an occasion to know how highly he thought of Aunt Clara—confirmed Rosie's gloomy announcement. "I've told your aunt repeatedly that this asthma of her isn't helped at all by San Francisco dampness. But you know how stubborn Miss Harwood can be. Of course, as a native San Franciscan myself"—here he permitted himself a faint smile—"I admire and sympathize with her love for this colorful old town. Just the same, my advice to you, Mrs. Caswell, is to persuade her to go somewhere like Arizona. That is, if you can budge her. Meanwhile, I want her to rest for a few days. No more of these women's board meetings or gadding about all over town. It wouldn't do her any harm to read a good book every now and again." He took a firmer grip on his medical satchel and nodded to me. "I'll drop by tomorrow afternoon after lunch."

"Dr. Hargrove, I've always known about her asthma, of course," I said as I walked down the stairway with him, "but this business about her heart is new, isn't it?"

"Not entirely, Mrs. Caswell, to be truthful with you. She's had all these years what we doctors call a nervous heart, in layman's language. And the constant coughing and the strain on her bronchial tubes from the asthma have put an extra strain on the heart muscles and the valves. Oh, don't misinterpret what I'm saying—she's in no great immediate danger. I'd like to see her rest and not be so high-strung, particularly about those social hen parties of hers. I'm afraid I don't have a very high medical opinion of their sanguinary effect." Again he showed a faint smile.

"I'll take good care of her, Doctor Hargrove, I promise. And Rosie, whether Aunt Clara likes it or not, will see to it that she gets exactly the menu you've prescribed. Thank you so much, Doctor."

I closed the door behind him, and as I stood there, a sudden anxiety totally replaced my earlier brief pleasure. I was going to have to tell Alan about Aunt Clara, and I was going to make a point of urging him to be especially nice to her. And

155

that was ironic, because of late he had been neglecting me as much as he had my aunt. He seemed to have become a totally changed person, with a driving force compelling him to concentrate on his work. We hadn't had dinner together for at least a week now, and he would often leave the house before I came down for breakfast. Even Aunt Clara had begun to make embarrassing comments to me about his sudden preoccupation with everything except his own wife. And the natural fear and concern I felt for the kindly woman who had brought me up from childhood were intensified by my own complete mystification over Alan Caswell's having relegated me to the very background of his life.

Chapter
FIFTEEN

AUNT CLARA stayed in bed for three or four days, until Dr. Hargrove grudgingly told her that it would be all right to be up and around provided she didn't overexert herself. And he told me to make sure that she didn't. Aunt Clara seemed more tired and docile than I had ever seen her before, but she still had energy enough to tell him that she wasn't exactly a baby and that she didn't need anyone to look after her. "If you keep up that attitude, Miss Harwood," he gave it right back to her, "you may wind up having a girl in a starched uniform looking after you and taking your temperature and doing other unpleasant things to you. Mrs. Caswell, I'd like you to call me every few days just to let me know how your aunt's getting along. And keep up that diet. I've written out a prescription for a little stimulant, which may help take away that feeling of exhaustion. Please see that she takes it."

I promised him that I'd do everything I could, and we left Aunt Clara's room while she continued to grumble about the unheard-of audacity and impertinence of the modern physician. When we reached the hallway, Dr. Hargrove gave me a sly look and commented, "Don't ever let your aunt know, but I think she's a remarkable woman. If all my patients were as healthily unneurotic as she is, my profession would really be a delight. Well, good morning, Mrs. Caswell."

I sent Rosie out to get the prescription and reminded her again that Aunt Clara was to have exactly the kind of food the doctor had ordered and that there were to be no snacks sent up to her on the sly. Rosie flushed, then looked reproachful, and I suspected that Aunt Clara had tried to induce her to bring forbidden treats to her room when I wasn't around. I said as much.

Rosie looked unhappy. "Well, ma'am, I will say she's been giving me lots of trouble and bawling me out about the slop—that's her very word, Mrs. Caswell, and you know I'm a better cook than that—that I've been feeding her. She's even said that if I didn't feed her right, she'd fire me."

I laughed and patted Rosie on the shoulder. "Don't worry, Rosie. Your job's safe. Just you do what I told you. You want Miss Harwood to be around with us for a long time, don't you?"

Rosie emphatically bobbed her head. "I sure do, Mrs. Caswell! She's a wonderful person, and I couldn't ask for a nicer place to work at. I'll do what you say, don't you worry." Then she gave me a supplicating look. "But if she does fire me, ma'am, you'll put in a good word for me?"

"I'll fire you myself if you don't hurry up and get that prescription filled, Rosie. And don't you worry. I'll be responsible for everything," I told her.

Aunt Clara welcomed the authorization to leave her bed, but it was plain that she was chafing under the restraint Dr. Hargrove had imposed. She also began to show an air of martyrdom that would have done credit to a Christian sent into the arena, and the next day I overheard her talking to one of the members of the opera fund-raising board in the most lugubrious tones, bewailing the fact that a tyrannical doctor had virtually made her a prisoner in her own house and that regrettably she would be unable to attend the dinner in Sausalito that evening. Somehow, I felt closer to her than I ever had; all these years she had been a tower of strength as my guardian and the only one to whom I could really turn. And strangely, now, though I had a husband whom I loved, I felt that I needed Aunt Clara and that, for perhaps the first time, she needed me, because of her illness.

It was a kind of compensation, too, because this unknown barrier between Alan and myself was persisting. I had already told him about Aunt Clara's illness and tactfully suggested that he go out of his way to be especially nice to her. He had blandly agreed, and on the occasions when the three of us sat down together for a meal—which continued to be infrequent—he did seem to make the effort to be pleasant and to keep a cheerful conversation

159

going. But he continued to be away from home several evenings a week, till ten or eleven o'clock, always with the excuse of doing extra work or having to visit a client in San Rafael or Burlingame. I didn't mind this, because he seemed to be somewhat more affectionate. At least, when he did come home in the evening and when he left in the morning, he kissed me in a way much more becoming to a newly married husband than he had the past few weeks. And the night of the same day that Dr. Hargrove had given me Aunt Clara's prescription, he made love to me after a long abstinence, and once again I felt myself completely his.

I told myself that if it hadn't been for Aunt Clara's illness, Alan and I might have gone away for the summer, perhaps back to Hawaii, where we had had our honeymoon and where we had known such flawless happiness. I reminded myself that he was proud and ambitious and that, as far as Aunt Clara was concerned, if not myself, he was trying to rid himself of the handicap of having been the grandson of the man who had quarreled with my grandfather. It was better, I told myself too, that both of us knew exactly where we stood, because then there could be no evasions or secrets between us. And I was certain that he wasn't involved with another woman. At least, I could detect no signs of that in either his appearance or his conduct.

Besides, I was engrossed with the project I had

set myself, to learn as much as I could about the Dade Navigation Company. In the morning, when Alan had gone to work, I would go up to the attic and read the diary-ledger, passing over the accounts of scandals and business coups in my search for passages that would show me how my grandfather had expanded the Dade fleet and what problems he had had to face in doing it. His writing was often difficult for me to read, quite apart from the faded ink, because when he was in a reflective mood, he seemed to write more doggedly in that small, cramped, old-fashioned penmanship which is seldom used today. Other times, when he was happy or feeling successful after engineering some piece of strategy over his competitors, he wrote with a bold and erratic flourish, which was equally difficult to decipher.

Yet that reference to the *Afrikander* and the mysterious square with its dots and dashes continued to titillate my curiosity. There was, of course, no one alive who could tell me anything about that ill-fated vessel or John Dade's salvaging of its precious cargo. And since he had said that he had effected that salvaging on his own and without involving the company, it was also unlikely that there would be any records kept in the old wooden file cabinets that I knew to be stored in a large closet at the end of the tenth floor in the Ferry Building. Mr. Pearson had told me that these cabinets contained documents prior to World War I and that, since they were almost never referred to, they had been locked away in a room all to themselves, more as historical and sentimental preservation than as necessary reference.

I could understand that my grandfather had made enemies. Able men who refuse to be swerved from achieving their goals inevitably do. Here and there throughout those faded pages which covered a period of about ten years, there were occasional laconic sentences or even uncompleted ones indicating that John Dade had met with hostility on the docks, as well as in his own office. Several times he had quelled uprisings with his own fists, then stood the malcontent a round of drinks to show that there were no hard feelings. The portrait of an indomitable man, albeit a lonely one, came to me after my many readings. My hiding place seemed safe, for I always found the trunk was always exactly as I had left it. Whenever I sat before the gabled window, glancing up from pages of a bygone era to see the surroundings of Telegraph Hill, I thought that somehow the surroundings were still the same, and there was more than ever a feeling of belonging, of identifying myself with my parents and with my grandfather who had created so much that thousands now could enjoy and profit from.

By the first week of September, Aunt Clara was already angrily declaring that she meant to resume her rounds of social activities, and I had Dr. Hargrove come over to examine her. He agreed that there was a small improvement but insisted that she conserve her strength, and she gave him a piece of her tongue, which could be sharp-edged when she was in the mood. He told her that her obstreperousness was a good sign indeed and commended her to my efficient caretaking.

Alan seemed to be more pleasant now, and occasionally he favored us with his presence at dinner. Rosie, who appeared to have been partly won over by his charm, managed to outdo herself on those occasions, and her culinary achievements were quite as good as any we might have enjoyed in the city's finest restaurants. To my surprise, she was even able to prepare an extremely tasty *coq au vin,* which even Alan himself pronounced the equal of any he had had at the Fleur de Lys.

The night before Labor Day was a particularly gloomy one. It had been raining most of the day, and by four that afternoon a heavy fog had settled down, coming in from the ocean and rapidly engulfing Golden Gate Park and very soon thereafter the rest of the city all the way down to the Embarcadero. Aunt Clara had reluctantly turned down an invitation to a soiree given by a socialite matron who was an officer of the symphony board of directors, and after dinner she excused herself with the comment that there wasn't much to do on a night like this except go to bed early.

Alan and I were alone in the big dining room, where Rosie had just served us a highly palatable roast duckling in orange sauce. Aunt Clara had, soon after moving in with me, purchased a small but carefully chosen selection of wines, and a special rack had been installed down in the old stone cellar to keep it properly stored. We had had an excellent bottle of Moselle, that Rhine wine which, in its great years, can be the match of any regal white Burgundy from France. Alan lifted his glass and smiled at me. "To you, Arlene, for putting up with me through this difficult summer," he said softly, and sipped his wine.

"Have I been a trying wife to you, darling?" I asked.

"No, I'm the one who's tried your patience, and I know it. I've been working like a dog, and there's a chance that I may become a partner in the investment house very soon."

"How wonderful, darling! Nothing could make me happier. And I know that you'll feel better too, once you've proved what you can do. But then you deserve it, you've been working so hard."

He nodded thoughtfully. "I've had a lot on my mind, Arlene. But I've never stopped loving you, even if I haven't always shown it."

I lifted my glass and smiled at him. "There's always a time of readjustment in a new marriage, Alan. The only hardship on me has been that I've thought I wasn't right for you, or maybe you were tired of me."

He left his chair and came around to mine, lifted me up, and kissed me. "Tired of you, you enchanting little devil?" he teased with that boyish little grin which always lowered my defenses. "That's impossible!" And then, gaily, he proposed, "Let's give Rosie a surprise and do the dishes ourselves, just as if we were a poor struggling young couple that couldn't afford a maid or a house like this."

And so that evening was bright in contrast to the ghostly fog that enshrouded our old house, and we laughed and chatted away in the kitchen, having sent Rosie off to her room. And when the dishes were done, he took me in his arms again and kissed me, and then I knew the joy of being a wife who loved and was loved. . . .

Concern over Alan's previous and unexplained neglect of me had caused me many a sleepless night. I had found myself waking with a start, at three or four in the morning, and this night—though it had culminated in a reassurance of his constancy for me—was no different. I suddenly found myself staring at the canopy overhead, and then vaguely I heard the tinkling sound of the little Swiss chime clock from the dining room, and my lips moved as I counted the hours it sounded off . . . one, two, three. I turned my head and I put out my arm for Alan, but the bed was empty. I smiled to myself, thinking how very wifely that gesture of mine had just been. It was a good augury, I told myself. But I wished he had been more confident in me, more certain of my trust in him. Then he could have told me about his many absences from home, made me a part of his plans to advance on his job, and I would have been happy to know I could share that with him. I made up my mind to ask him to take me into his confidence, so that there could be nothing hidden between us.

From afar I heard the distant forghorns near Alcatraz Island. That was a landmark of our city. In my father's time, it was the top-security prison for the most hardened and dangerous criminals. Now the prison buildings stood, lonely and deserted, out in the fog. And it had always been a legend that no convict had ever escaped from that gloomy prison and managed the slightly more than a mile swim through freezing waters and dangerous tides and even sharks. The legend would still be preserved now for all time to come.

I closed my eyes, my mind still in that drowsy torpor between sleep and waking, and I thought of little excursions and holidays that Alan and I might take this fall. And then there came a sound that I could not quite identify. It sounded like the clinking of a metallic object; yet it was muffled. I waited, and it came again, and then again after a prolonged interval, and then again and again and again, and then it stopped. Perhaps it was the old waterpipes or something in the furnace. Then there was nothing to worry about, because old Henry Jennings was certain to repair whatever flaw there was. And with a sigh, I drifted off again to sleep.

Chapter
SIXTEEN

THAT NEXT week Alan stayed at home and was a model husband in every respect. He went out only once, to a Wednesday appointment in San Mateo. He was playfully gallant toward Aunt Clara—he held her chair for her at the dining table and made little jokes about her improved health and her cantankerous temper. I saw that she rather enjoyed it, though of course, she didn't let on to him. But during that week, on two other nights when I wakened before dawn, I found Alan gone, and again I heard that puzzling clinking sound. On Friday night—or rather, Saturday morning— I could not go right back to sleep, and I lay there waiting and thinking and listening to the little Swiss clock chime four. Just as the last overtone died away, Alan came back into the bedroom, in his bathrobe and pajamas. "I missed you, darling," I murmured, holding out my arms to him. He bent to crush out his cigarette in the little ashtray on the night table, then clambered into bed beside me. "Some nights I can't sleep, Arlene dear," he explained as he held me close to him and kissed my eyelids and the tip of my nose, which I always adored his doing. "I guess I'm so wrought up over my job that I've drawn myself rather fine. So I go off walking through the house—sometimes, if it isn't too cold and foggy at night, I even stroll through the garden, just thinking and planning. Don't you worry, though; in a little while everything will be fine. I'll have what I want, and then you'll be proud of me."

"Alan, no job's worth killing yourself for. I love you as you are, not because you're going to be partner in a big, important firm. Didn't you once say that you'd love me even if I were King Cophetua's beggar-maid?"

"Of course I did. And I meant it. Now let's go to sleep."

All through that Labor Day week we had a siege of fog, starting in late afternoon, so thick and clinging that sometimes even by early morning it still lingered. The temperature dropped at least fifteen to twenty-five degrees between midafternoon and night, and the weather definitely curtailed Aunt Clara's would-be social activities, much to my relief. She had begun again to issue ultimatums about refusing to continue such a sedentary life.

I visited the offices of the Dade Navigation Company the following Tuesday afternoon, and Mr. Pearson and Mr. Wales took me into the conference room. The deal with the San Pedro ship-owner had been consummated, Mr. Pearson informed me, and some of our engineers and commissary executives were down there now inspecting the ships and making plans to remodel them so that they might carry passengers as well as cargo.

"So you see, Mrs. Caswell," Mr. Pearson said, beaming, "that was a first-rate idea of yours, and it's going to be put into operation just as soon as feasible. As a matter of fact, one of the ships we've just added to the Dade fleet in this latest transaction of ours is docked at Pier Three. Perhaps you'd like to see it after you leave here?"

"I'd like that very much, Mr. Pearson."

He glanced at Adam Wales, gave the latter a broad wink, then turned to me with an expansive smile. "We've taken the liberty—with your permission, I do hope, and with no thought of presumption on our part—of changing the name to the *Arlene*."

"I'm very flattered, and you certainly have my permission," I laughed, "but don't forget, Mr. Pearson, that a woman is a fickle, changeable, and sometimes illogical creature, and I only hope that giving a good ship my name won't jinx her."

William Pearson shook his head. "I'm a plainspeaking man at all times, Mrs. Caswell. Frankly, when I first learned that you were going to inherit the company, I told myself that we might all expect some drastic changes. Young people these days don't have much patience with tradition and responsibility and the like. You could have certainly been well within your rights to sell, and you'd have made a very striking profit, judging from this market quotation on our stock. But the way you've taken an interest in what's going on here has heartened all of us, Mrs. Caswell. We feel you're one of the family—a real Dade, just like your father and your grandfather before him."

I blushed at this and stammered something about still having a great deal to learn and intending, with their help, to learn it. Then I shook hands with them and left the office. A cab parked in front of the Ferry Building took me along the Embarcadero to Pier 3. I paid the driver and told him not to wait, and then I walked toward the ship. On the hull, I could see the words *The Arlene* brightly shining, and I think I can be pardoned the stimulus to my ego that that sight gave me. It was a sturdy freighter, and I could foresee that though it would never be another *Asturia*, it could be made quite comfortable for perhaps a dozen or twenty people who could visit exciting foreign ports on a modest budget. I walked about, from this side to that, admiring the ship, watching the stevedores unload her. The air was chilly again, and the sky was murky. Soon the fog would move in from the Bay and hide all these ships along the wharfs till they became a ghostly armada. But this armada was one of peace and vital commerce, not a hostile assault upon our shores.

Suddenly I heard a cry, "Look out! The cable's loose!" And then, before I knew what was happening, somebody had grabbed me and was lifting me up and running with me; before I could object or struggle, I heard a crash behind me. I turned my head back over the man's shoulder and saw a huge steamship trunk flattened and broken open on the wharf, on the very spot where I had just been standing.

"That was a close one, Miss!" A young, curly-brown-haired, sturdy man in the work shoes and denim overalls of a stevedore grinned at me. I felt my knees give way beneath me in nervous reaction, and I swayed. "Hey, now, take it easy, take it easy! It's all right now!" he exclaimed as he slid an arm around my waist and supported me.

I closed my eyes and let the waves of nausea recede. Yes, it had been much too close. If he hadn't done what he did, I'd have been killed. "Th-thank you. You saved my life. And it was my fault for being so wrapped up in what I was looking at that I didn't notice the unloading cranes on the next ship."

"Sure, I understand, Miss. Ever since I was a kid, I've loved ships and I guess I've come down here to stare at them just the way you were doing. Do you feel better now?"

I nodded, still feeling my heart pound, and I knew that I was pale with the shock of aftermath.

"You're very brave. You yourself might have been killed. Thank God it didn't happen."

"Best forget about it, Miss. You seem to like that old freighter a lot, hm?"

I was suddenly garrulous, again a natural reaction after my fright. Also, I felt I owed him an explanation. Why, he surely wondered, did a giddy female stand looking at a freighter without even knowing what was going on around her? "You see, that freighter has my name on it. The *Arlene*. And I guess that's the first ship I've ever seen my own name on."

"Well, now, that explains it. I guess I'd be lost in admiration if I saw my own name on a ship. How about a cup of coffee? My name's Ron Jennings."

"And mine's Arlene Dade."

His cheery smile momentarily left his friendly, freckled, and weatherbeaten face, and his blue eyes narrowed. "Arlene Dade?" he repeated. "The one who came into the Dade Navigation Company a little while back?"

"Guilty as charged. I'm Wilson Dade's daughter."

"Now isn't that something!" He uttered a low whistle. "It's funny how things work out sometimes, isn't it?"

"Why, yes. But what do you mean, Mr. Jennings?"

"Skip the 'Mr. Jennings,' if you don't mind.

The name's Ron. I'm a union stevedore, and I'm not an executive or a big boss, though I might make assistant foreman if I try real hard." He grinned as he took hold of my arm and led me to a little waterfront café. "What I meant was, my dad used to play with your dad when the both of them were kids."

"Jennings—yes, of course!" I exclaimed. "Old Henry Jennings is the caretaker of our house on Union Street. And he was telling me about his brother Luke and that Luke had a son named Gregory—"

"He was my dad, Miss Dade. He and Mom died last year in a plane crash over in Europe. They'd always wanted to see Europe, you know. I put aside some of my wages down here so they could have that trip. I wish to hell I hadn't."

He looked away, his face twisted with a momentary grief, and I hesitantly touched his arm. "I'm sorry."

He took a deep breath and then smiled again. We sat down at the counter, and he ordered two Boston coffees. I had no intention of changing that to black, because it would have been far too ungracious after what Ron Jennings had just done. "Sure, my Dad used to play in the garden with Willy—that's what he called your dad, Miss Dade."

"Yes. My lawyer, Douglas Murray, told me."

"From what Dad used to tell me, your old man

173

was sort of lonesome. I mean, they kept him from playing with the other kids in the neighborhood and I guess just about kept him locked up in that old house because he was going to grow up and take over the Dade Company, hm?"

"Yes. I'm afraid that's about it. And I've double reason to be grateful to you then, Ron. Not only did you save my life just now, but your father helped my father forget some of the loneliness of that old house. I think I know what it can be like."

"So you're living back in it now, Miss Dade?"

"Yes You know, my parents died when I was not quite eleven, and then my aunt and I lived out on the Avenues till this year. And my father's will required that I go back to live on Union Street."

"It's sure funny how time changes things and yet doesn't quite, isn't it, Miss Dade?"

"Now if I'm going to call you Ron, I insist that you call me Arlene. I certainly don't feel very mature and grown-up, not after standing under that crane and not even knowing what was happening."

"Sure. I'd like to. Want some more coffee?"

"No, thanks very much. I guess I'd better be getting back home now, Ron. But I'll come down to the docks again. Only the next time, I'll take a safer vantage place from which to look at my ship."

"You just do that now, Arlene." He rose and

held the door of the café open for me, tipping his cap. He was a little like Jim Kinsolving, I thought. And then I rebuked myself for that reminder of what should have been dead and buried long in the past.

"It's told along the waterfront that your company's just bought out some freighters out of San Pedro," Ron Jennings said. "Come on along and I'll get you a cab. It's not going to be easy this time of late afternoon. And the fog's starting to come down again. It's a good thing we finished unloading."

"It's a good thing for me you weren't busy at the time, I can tell you that!" I exclaimed with a nervous laugh. "Yes, it's true about those ships, Ron. The one with my name on it is part of that fleet. Mr. Pearson, our sales manager, told me that he had had it renamed in my honor. I'm beginning to wonder, as I told him back in the office, if that wasn't going to jinx it. Just see how very nearly I jinxed it for fair!"

He'd seen a cruising cab and with a piercing whistle, putting two fingers to his lips—a trick I've always envied and have never been able to emulate—flagged it down for me. As he helped me in, he said, "It's going to be a lucky ship, Arlene. You watch and see. And I'll be looking for you down here again. Maybe I can buy you a lunch. I'll say one thing, though."

"And what's that, Ron?"

175

He grinned and winked at me. "Never in a million years will that ship be as pretty as you are. And I'm sure glad I saved you. This town needs all the pretty girls it has, believe you me. Well, see you again then."

Chapter
SEVENTEEN

ALAN HAD left word with Rosie that he wouldn't be back till late that night, since he had a dinner engagement with a client in Tiburon. And I found Aunt Clara in a towering rage, pacing back and forth in the living room and ready to pounce on me as soon as Rosie had delivered her message.

"Where in the world have you been, Arlene?" she demanded. "Mr. Pearson called me nearly two hours ago saying that you'd left the office and might go down to the wharf to see that new boat they named after you. I thought for a while they might have shanghaied you."

"It's not a boat, dear, it's a ship. And I wasn't shanghaied, but I was rescued."

"And what do you mean by that bit of double talk?"

"I did go down there to see the *Arlene*, and I was so proud and I guess maybe so vain that I didn't see a crane lifting a trunk over my head. And the cable snapped, and one of the stevedores nearby saw what was happening and pulled me out of the way. And we had coffee together and we talked. And I guess I'm still a little shaken."

"Well, I should think so! But you're not the only one."

"And now it's my turn to ask you what you mean, Aunt Clara."

"Then I'll tell you. That husband of yours is up to something. I'm not quite sure what, but he's been a little too changeable to suit me. Maybe you're still mooning over him, and that's your business, but I told you I had my doubts about him the minute you said his name was Caswell. You remember that private investigator I used to check his background?"

"Yes, I do. And you had nothing to worry about, as I recall."

"That's true. But all these sudden business appointments that keep him out after dinner until late at night, they've had me wondering for quite some time now. So I had the investigator do some checking again last week."

"But last week, Alan was home most of the time."

"Except Wednesday. You remember he said he was going out to San Mateo. He did, all right. And he went to the house of a Miss Ellen Wilbur, whose parents happen to be in Europe right now and who is, according to my investigator, a redhead who'd have no trouble getting a job in a topless-waitress establishment. Her parents happen to be the Clark Wilburs, the sugar people."

"Well," I said lamely, "perhaps, since she's probably wealthy in her own right, she's speculating with Allan's firm."

"Speculating with Alan, more likely. They were in there three hours before he came out, and he was rearranging his tie and smoothing that sleek black hair of his."

"I can't understand why you're spying on him. And I don't think I like it, Aunt Clara."

"Well, for one thing, Doctor Hargrove keeps saying I have to keep out of all my nice board meetings, so you can't blame me if I try to keep myself occupied." She looked at me with a searching, anxious stare now, and her voice was graver. "There's something else you don't know."

"Then tell me."

"This afternoon, while you were over at the office, Alan came back home for lunch. He was in a foul mood, too, I can tell you. And he was saying that you and I didn't trust him and that just because his name was Caswell, the two of us were down on him from the very start. I told him that I'd had him investigated and that everything had seemed to be perfectly satisfactory, and that was why I hadn't opposed the marriage. And you loved him, I said, even if lately he didn't seem to appreciate it very much."

"Aunt Clara! You shouldn't have told him that!"

"But I did. I want things out in the open. And

he shouldn't have anything to hide, either, not like that Ellen Wilbur."

"You mean you confronted him with that, too?"

Aunt Clara nodded. "He didn't say anything. He just looked at me and shook his head. And then he went on to say that it wasn't fair for a grandson to have to answer for his grandfather's misdeeds and that if there was only some tangible proof that his grandfather hadn't been in the wrong, all this would be different and he wouldn't be living under this burden. And that's when I told him about the diary."

"The diary?" I echoed, thunderstruck.

"Yes. That big leather-bound book with the clasp. I said that John Dade had written it and that if his grandfather Henry Caswell had been a thieving rogue, it would have been down there once and for all. And I told him that of course, I wasn't blaming him for anything his grandfather might or mightn't have done, I just wanted the two of you to be happy, and I wasn't so sure that you were."

"Well, at least the air should be clear," I said with a long sigh. "I think we'd better have supper and then play some cribbage and settle our nerves. And I'll apologize to Alan."

"You'll do nothing of the sort!" Aunt Clara said firmly. "There's nothing to apologize for. I just told him I'd like to know more about Miss Ellen Wilbur and what kind of business she can be doing with his company. I happen to know that her trust fund's tied up till she's twenty-five, because she's a wild one, with quite a reputation even back in high school. And I doubt very much that her parents would allow her to speculate with their money. My advice to you, dear, is to go along and made the best of things, but just keep your eyes open. And I'll be glad to let my private investigator work for you and check up to see whether your husband is doing a little philandering after hours."

We played cribbage until nearly eleven o'clock, and Aunt Clara was visibly exhausted. Alan still hadn't come home, and my own near-fatal adventure that afternoon had left me still shaken and nervous. I decided to take a sleeping pill and go to bed. Since Alan had come to live with us, Rosie had been moved to an upstairs room on the opposite side of the landing, using the one next to my old room. The house was quiet. Only the vague, mournful wail of the foghorn broke the stillness. I was asleep before I knew it. . . .

There was a noise that kept persisting, growing louder and louder, even as I mumbled, "What is it—I'm coming—I hear you." I blinked my eyes and adjusted myself. The noise continued, a hammering at the door. Alan sat up beside me in the bed. "What the devil's that!" he exclaimed, and got out of bed and put on his bathrobe over his pajamas.

Still dazed, I groped for my slippers and then my robe and followed him. He opened the door to find Rosie, tears streaming down her face, wringing her hands in a state of near hysteria. "It's Miss Harwood, it's Miss Harwood!" she cried, "I can't wake her. I just took up her breakfast, and she's lying there so still, and I put my hand on her heart and I can't feel a beat, oh please, Mr. Caswell, come look at her!"

"Now, now, Rosie, suppose you go call Doctor Hargrove right away, and my wife and I will go right up to her," Alan soothed her. She dabbed at her eyes with the corner of her apron, nodded, and hurried off to the phone.

"Alan, I'm afraid," I gasped. "That asthma of hers and the heart condition—do you suppose— oh, God, no!"

"Now get a grip on yourself, Arlene." He came over to me and put his arm around my shoulders, kissing me on the cheek. "Don't go to pieces like Rosie. We'll go see right now."

"Yes, Alan. I went to sleep last night without you—you must have been very late coming home."

"It was after midnight, darling. I'm sorry. But let's find out what's the matter."

When we entered Aunt Clara's room, I recoiled with a sobbing cry. She lay, half-twisted on her back, her hands drawn up and clenched in fists at her chest, her head tilted back and her eyes staring. Alan quickly bent to her, grasped one of her limp wrists and felt for her pulse. Then slowly he turned to me and shook his head. "She's dead, darling."

"Oh, dear God!" I burst into tears. "And we never knew! If only I could have been with her! We played cribbage, and she said she was tired and was going to sleep. And then I took a sleeping pill, because I was so exhausted too. And—and maybe when you came in . . ." I couldn't finish.

His arms were around me, and he was trying to soothe me, to tell me that I mustn't blame myself. Then he went downstairs to get me a drink of brandy and made me swallow nearly half of it. Rosie had phoned Dr. Hargrove, and when he arrived half an hour later, he said to us, "I warned her not to overdo things. I had hoped that by keeping her here in the house and not letting her gad about so much, this wouldn't happen. It's a heart attack, Mrs. Caswell. The combination of that with her chronic asthma was just too much. I feel such a sense of loss at this."

Dazed with grief, I hardly heard Alan talking to him to make what necessary arrangements must be done at such a time. All I could think of was that the exertion Dr. Hargrove had feared might well have been that quarrel between Aunt Clara and my husband. And I hadn't been there to prevent it, thinking only of myself and of my name on the ship. And in a way, I couldn't help thinking that I had been responsible for Aunt Clara's death.

Chapter
EIGHTEEN

ALL THE WEEK of Aunt Clara's funeral, Alan was quiet and compassionate with me. And all that week the weather was as mournful as my own thoughts, with the fog surging in from the ocean and cloaking the entire city with its eerie mist. On the Monday after the funeral, while Alan was at work, I went up to the attic to find my grandfather's diary-ledger. I read it and reread it until poor distracted Rosie had had to climb up the stairs and bang on the door to summon me urgently to lunch.

I don't know what decided me to copy that curious square with all its dots and dashes. Perhaps it was the remembrance of what Aunt Clara had said to me just before she died, about Alan's wishing that there were some written evidence of the past to exculpate his name. But I know that when Rosie summoned me and I finally acceded to her supplication that I come down to have a bite to eat because I looked so peaked, I forgot to put the ledger in the bottom of the old trunk. Absently,

I laid it down on a little footstool just inside the door. And that afternoon I went down to the docks again, like a lost soul seeking some link between the past and the present, something that would be less tenuous than the fog. Ron Jennings was there unloading another freighter, and he tipped his cap to me, went over to his foreman to ask for a few moments' leave, and then came to meet me with an outstretched hand.

"I have to offer my condolences, Arlene. I read about your aunt. A terrible thing. It's been hard on you, I can see that."

"Thank you, Ron. You've worked at the docks quite some time, haven't you?"

"Yes, ever since I left high school. But that's not to say I've just got a strong back and a weak mind, now." He grinned. "I'll have you know I've taken college courses at night, and I've even got myself a B.A. in commerce. Someday, maybe, I'll go to work in an office that has to do with ships. But right now, I like this outdoor life and the hard work. Gives a man a good appetite and a clear mind."

"My grandfather and my father thought so too, Ron. Do you know very much about the sea? I mean, about signals and naval codes and things?"

"Well, I know the Morse code and the international code. I wouldn't mind sailing on one of those really big ships like the *Asturia*. Of course, I'd need a lot of experience before they'd put me in charge of a beauty like that. Or even the beauty that's got your name on it, Arlene."

It was the first time I had laughed in longer than I could remember. He was refreshingly honest. And there was more to it than that. I owed him my life. And I owed him a debt of thanks for the kindness his father had shown my father when they were children. I had no one whom I could take into my confidence now. No, not even Alan. It was all a strange, unreasonable dream now, and I could only wait to see what its wakening would be like—if there was to be wakening from it and its tenuous, shadowy riddles.

I opened my old purse—I'd never replaced it after that afternoon when it had nearly been stolen —and I took out the slip of paper and handed it to Ron Jennings. "Can I ask you a favor?"

"Ask away, Arlene."

"My grandfather kept a diary covering about ten years up to the big earthquake. And there was something in that diary about the *Afrikander*. It was a ship that came from Mexico, and a former Spanish nobleman was carrying with him a great fortune in gold and jewels. The *Afrikander* was wrecked off the Monterey coast, and my grandfather wrote that he proposed to salvage it. He said that he wouldn't use the Dade company's men or equipment but would do it himself so that he could have that treasure as a kind of legacy for his own future in case anything ever happened to the company and made him penniless. And then there isn't anything else except this curious drawing. The more I've thought about it, Ron, the more I've thought it might be some kind of seaman's code. That's why I thought maybe you could decipher it."

He held it close, for the fog was thickening. "Mighty interesting," he finally commented. "Yes, you're right, it's something like the Morse code— I could tell that right away—but it's not that easy."

"Will you take it and study it and see what you can learn for me?" I pleaded.

"Of course, Arlene."

"If it leads me to that treasure, needless to say you'll have your share."

"I'm not doing it for that, Arlene. You don't need to promise anything. And now I've got to get back to work."

"I'll come down to the docks again in a few days," I promised. "And I'm very grateful to you."

He turned back to give me that irrepressible grin of his and to call, "You've rewarded me enough just by coming down here, Arlene. The boys are going to be razzing me for days now to find out how I rate knowing a stunner like you."

He waved to me, then strode away. And somehow I felt my terrible weight of anxiety and guilt lifted, if only for a merciful moment.

I got home to find that Rosie had prepared an early dinner for us. Alan had telephoned to say that he wished to take me to *La Traviata* at the opera and would dine at home. Oddly enough, I hadn't been aware of Alan's interests in music. To be sure, we'd listened and danced to popular music and he'd indicated some of his favorites, and occasionally he'd listen to FM in the evening, but he'd never mentioned liking opera. Moreover, this archaic masterpiece with its story of true love and renunciation was a bit too saccharine for my tastes. Yet his wish to escort me was a welcome sign.

I had Rosie help me on with a new off-the-shoulder evening formal that Aunt Clara had bought me as a part of my trousseau. It was the first time I'd worn that thoughtful gift, and as I studied my reflection in the mirror, I felt tears rise to my eyes. How I wish she could have come with us tonight! Her steadying influence might have helped solidify our marriage, about which I had begun to have grave misgivings.

Alan drove his Impala to the War Memorial Opera House and had the doorman park it for us. Offering me his arm, he swept through the admiring crowds with the air of a *grand seigneur,* and flash bulbs popped amid excited gossip as the newspaper photographers took our photos for the society section.

We had a box, I found to my surprise—I would have preferred less prominence—and Alan brought me a box of chocolates to nibble on. His attentiveness, his striking good looks, his flawless manners were, I knew, the cynosure of all eyes.

And toward the end of the first act, I was already restless, wanting it to be over. Violetta's problems seemed somehow centuries remote and in no way helpful toward the solution of my own.

When the curtain fell, Alan applauded, turning to me to comment how much he had enjoyed it and how he was looking forward to the great death scene when the elder Germont comes to tell Violetta that he has misjudged her and at last withdraws his objection to her marriage with his son. I glanced at him with astonishment, and as if he had read my mind, he whispered with a mocking little smile, "You're forgetting, Arlene dear, that there's still a great deal about me you don't know. But that's the fun of being married, isn't it?" And then he leaned back, folding his arms with the evident relish of a connoisseur of Verdi as the lyrical prelude to the second act began.

At last it was over, but strangely, Alan was in no hurry to leave. He led the applause for the conductor and then the stars, and only when the lights of that huge chandelier—which I can never look at without the shuddering premonition that it will fall at any moment!—went on did he bow to me with the air of a gallant who prepares to escort his lady to her dwelling.

Still more surprisingly, though he knew that I never indulge in a late snack after dinner—and Rosie's way with a pork loin roast and sweet potatoes had been amply satisfying—he suggested that we stop at the Buena Vista on Taylor for Irish coffee and a sandwich. When I hesitated, he coaxed me by saying that it was the first night out the two of us had had for some time and he was reluctant to bring it to an end. And so, as always under the spell of his charm, which he knew so well how to turn on, I capitulated.

It was well after one in the morning when we at last arrived at the old house on Union Street, and Alan parked the Impala while I went ahead, for I was suddenly very tired. Rosie, of course, went to bed every night almost religiously at ten, and she claimed that she could sleep through an earthquake. Happily, thus far there had been no such occurrence to test the veracity of that assertion. Indeed, since the big tremor in March 1957, we had had very few scares, though there had been an occasional minor tremor in Contra Costa County.

I quickly undressed and went straight to bed, while Alan lingered in the living room, savoring a glass of sherry and smoking a cigarette. He had said that the opera and the outing with me had exhilarated him and that he didn't have to go to the office the next morning, since he had a luncheon date with a client and would drive to Oakland directly from the house. So he came into the bedroom to kiss me good night and then went out, leaving the door just ajar. Tired though I was, I had half-expected that he would make love to me, the natural consequence of so pleasant an evening. And Aunt Clara's remark about Ellen Wilbur suddenly filtered back into my drowsy mind, and then the name of Patricia Mallers, that school chum he had gone to see at the airport—or so Aunt Cllara had thought. Angrily, I forced myself to stop thinking, and, closing my eyes, I gradually felt myself falling asleep.

Once again—restless, no doubt, from all the subconscious anxieties that I had not succeeded in driving out of my thoughts—I woke to find myself alone in the four-poster bed. The door was nearly wide-open, and I heard the little Swiss clock chime four times. I sighed and turned over onto my other side, drawing the covers up about me, and then that strange, vague clinking sound I had heard before seemed to follow on the last tone of the final chime. There was a pause, and then the sound was repeated several times, quickly, as if someone were hammering on stone. And then it stopped.

I lay there listening, my heart beating quickly. There was silence now. And then, just as I thought I might fall back into longed-for sleep, I heard another sound, one that made me shudder and clutch the covers against me with a convulsive grasp. The sound of moaning, and then—how uncannily and terribly—the sound of the plash of water, like the sound waves make against a rowboat out in the Bay. Then this too was silent, and again the moaning resumed. I sat up in bed, perspiration breaking out on my forehead, and I called out, "Alan! Alan, where are you?"

And then suddenly, as if a ghost were stalking the old house, the sound of the lapping of waves came again, but this time in the bedroom itself, all around me. And then, after it had quieted, while I sat congealed in terror, that dreadful moaning, which seemed to be that of a man in agony, came again. This sound too seemed to surround me. I shrieked Alan's name, imploring him to come to me.

And then there was silence, and a few moments later Alan, in bathrobe and pajamas, hurried to my side and took me in his arms. "Darling, what's the matter? Were you having a bad dream?"

Falteringly, I told him what I had heard, but he laughed gently and shook his head. "You're mistaken, darling. I was in the library reading—I guess I shouldn't have had that sandwich after all —and I heard nothing except the little clock chime the hour. Now forget all about it like a good girl, and let's go to sleep."

Chapter
NINETEEN

I SLEPT TILL noon the next day, and Rosie's solicitous chatter about how I had enjoyed the opera
and whom I had seen there helped me put aside
the inexplicable and terrifying experience I had
had. Knowing that Alan would probably not be
back till evening, I decided to go to the docks and
see Ron Jennings again to learn whether he had
had an opportunity to study the mysterious cipher
I had discovered in my grandfather's diary-ledger.

The thought occurred to me that he might have
lost or misplaced the slip of paper on which I had
copied it, so I decided to go up to the attic and
refer to the book again and make another copy
for myself. After a hearty brunch, which further
helped to dispel the unpleasant and unexplained
episode, I went upstairs and opened the lid of the
trunk. As I lifted up the empty bottom drawer,
I stifled a gasp of surprise—the diary-ledger wasn't
there! And then I recalled that I had left it on top
of the trunk the last time I had gone to the attic.

Going back to the kitchen, I casually asked
Rosie if she had seen the leather-bound book any-

where in the house while she was dusting, but she said she had never seen such a book. I thanked her and had her pour me another cup of coffee. Then, in my most casual tone of voice, I asked whether she had heard anything unusual last night, and this too she emphatically denied.

It was very strange. What could have happened to John Dade's diary-ledger? Had Alan found it and decided to read it? Yes, that was certainly possible—but he would have had to go upstairs to the attic to find it on top of the trunk. And to the best of my knowledge, he had never gone up there.

I remembered now how Aunt Clara, on the last day of her life, had told me that he had been so insistent in finding some record from the past which would clear his grandfather's name. I could not really blame him if he had come across that book and, discovering what it was, decided to find out for himself what my grandfather had thought of Henry Caswell. And the only accusations I myself had found against Alan's grandfather had been John Dade's one angry invective against Henry Caswell's extravagance and profligacy. That and an earlier reference, dating back to 1898, that had referred to my grandfather's playing poker and losing the house to Henry Caswell and becoming his tenant and, four years later, a terse sentence, "I have won back my house because Caswell can't seem to hold on to his money."

Well, if Alan had found the book, he was welcome to it, I thought. But I meant to ask him about it when he came home. I told Rosie I was going downtown to do some shopping, and then I phoned for a cab. I directed the driver to take me to the Embarcadero, and I walked down to the dock where I had met Ron Jennings. However, he wasn't there, so I went up to the man who seemed to be the foreman and asked where I might find him. I was told that Ron had the day off and would be back tomorrow. Seeing my disappointment, the foreman, a swarthy Italian, winked and said, "If you like, *bella signorina,* I give you his phone number, eh?"

I hesitated, divining that he thought I was trying to make an amorous assignation. But I wanted to talk to Ron, so I overcame my squeamishness and thanked him for the number. Walking back to the little café where Ron and I had had coffee that afternoon he had saved me from the falling trunk, I dialed his number from the pay phone. And I felt an irrational pleasure when he answered.

His apartment was on Green Street, so I took a cab there and walked up to the second floor. He was already waiting on the threshold, having seen me alight from the cab. And the sight of his pleasant face somehow seemed to lift my spirits.

It was a small bachelor's apartment but remarkably neat and clean, and I teasingly commented on this. "Well, Arlene," he chuckled, "after all,

I'm a caretaker's son, and I'd better be a model housekeeper. I might have to go into that line of work someday if my muscles ever give out down at the docks."

"That's not very likely. Besides, with your studying nights, I'm sure you're headed for better things. Ron, I know I didn't give you much time, but were you able to do anything with that code I gave you the other day?"

He frowned. "Tell you the truth, I thought I had it, but I was all wet. But it's a variation of the Morse code, all right—that much I'm sure of. The trick is to find out how your grandfather reversed it and added to it. I was just going to start on it now, as a matter of fact. Can I make you some coffee?"

"No, thanks. I'll give you my phone number so you can call me if you work the code out. Rosie —my maid—will take a message for me if I'm not in. But . . . well, I'd rather you didn't talk to my husband if he answers the phone."

"Is he the jealous type?" he asked with a grin.

"It's not that, Ron. I—there's a lot I can't tell you. Except that he's the grandson of a man who used to be my grandfather's partner. There was bad blood between the two, and now I'm beginning to wonder if my husband isn't trying to find out about the past."

"Why don't you tell me the whole story? Then if I work out this code, I'll have a much better idea of what's going on."

I looked at him for a moment. Yes, I had to trust him. And I owed him at least the same honesty I'd given Alan at the start—perhaps more, for Ron Jennings had saved my life with his quick thinking. And so, drawing a long breath and sitting down on the couch beside him, I told him as briefly as I could how I had met Alan Caswell, how Aunt Clara had told me about his grandfather, and then how I had been given John Dade's old record book and learned of the reason for the quarrel between the two men.

"Now I begin to get the drift a little better, Arlene. Your grandfather most likely hired a free crew to work the salvage of the *Afrikander*, as a private operation. That meant he didn't have to turn any part of it over to the company or his partner. And that's what got Henry Caswell mad. And I think you're right in figuring that maybe that cipher tells where your grandfather hid what he found aboard the *Afrikander*."

"I'm more certain now than ever, Ron. And today when I went to look for my grandfather's book, it was missing; yet I left it in the attic and nobody else goes there. Perhaps my husband found it and is reading it to find out what went on between John Dade and his grandfather."

"That could very well be, Arlene. Then I'll keep at it, and I'll call you just as soon as I'm on to something."

I rose and held out my hand. "Thanks so much for all you've done."

"Sure." He shook hands with me and walked with me to the door. "I hope everything works out well for you, Arlene. You deserve the best."

"No." I shook my head. "I have to earn it first. Goodbye, and thanks again."

At dinner that evening, I tried to be casual with Alan all through the meal, to see if he would mention having found the book. He was congenial, in a more amiable mood than he had been the past few weeks, but his conversation touched only on his successful sale to the client he had lunched with, the weather—which was still foggy—and his enjoyment of the opera, with the hope that we might go again soon.

And so, after Rosie had cleared away the dishes and brought us our coffee, I took the bull by the horns and bluntly asked, "Alan, I've been looking for an old ledger that my grandfather had. It was sent to me by our family's attorney. Have you seen it?"

He set down his coffee cup, and a curious little smile wreathed his lips. "Yes, I have, as it happens, Arlene. You know, your Aunt Clara told me about that book. A kind of diary, wasn't it? The moment she told me, I knew I had to read it to find out what went on between my grandfather and John Dade."

"Then you've read it?"

He nodded, then deliberately took out a pack of cigarettes, chose one, and lit it. "Thoroughly.

The handwriting's hard to read, I'll admit, but it's very illuminating. Your grandfather was a shrewd man, Arlene, who wanted to keep one step ahead of everybody else."

"That doesn't mean he was dishonest."

Alan shrugged. "Who's to say by any standard? My grandfather thought he was, and I find he didn't have too high an opinion of my grandfather in turn. It rubbed off both ways. But what interests me is that reference to the *Afrikander*. My father once told me that John Dade and his father quarreled over the salvaging of a sunken ship and about the salvage rights. That was the ship, Arlene. And I'm convinced that your grandfather found the treasure and hid it. The blank page with that square and all its symbols—it might be a clue, don't you think?"

He looked up at me so blandly and calmly that I suddenly trembled. For his eyes were appraising and cold, as if I were a person who stood in his way, not the woman he professed to love. "Well?" he asked as his eyes fixed me with that unwavering stare.

"Y-yes, it might. I hadn't thought about it."

"Hadn't you? No, perhaps not," he drawled. "You're rich enough without adding treasure that's two generations old. But I'm not, and that's why it concerns me, too."

"What do you mean, Alan?"

"I mean that I need money, Arlene. I've been playing the market on margin, and I've got to raise a good deal to meet it or I'll be ruined and lose my job. You're my wife. Under California law, it's share and share alike."

And there it was, out in the open, naked and ugly, blighting all the joy we had known and shared at the outset of our marriage. And yet I felt relieved to know what had been troubling him so, making him moody and unpredictable. So I said, "Darling, you haven't been very well informed. Yes, it's share and share alike after the marriage. But if you thought when you married me that you'd automatically get half of everything that was willed to me, you were wrong. Wrong and cruel if you did that, Alan."

"No, no." Now he was suavely smiling. "I know the law as much as you do, my pet. It's half and half of what you get from now on, of course. And that means the *Afrikander* treasure. Only, I need it all, whatever it is, Arlene." And then the smile left his face and there was entreaty in his gaze. "What difference can it make to you, who have so much? I told you on the *Asturia* I wanted to stand on my own two feet, be able to support you and make a life for you. And that money doesn't really belong to you or John Dade, but to my grandfather—or at least a partner's share of it."

"Neither you nor I can be the one to decide that, Alan. We don't know the truth. Of course I'll help you, though, if you need money. But why didn't you ask me for it long before this?"

200

His face darkened with anger. "Because I'll not have it said I'm a kept man and doled out an allowance by a rich heiress, that's why!"

"That was a vicious thing to say," I stammered, feeling the flush of anger and shame burn my cheeks.

"No, it was the truth. Then you won't tell me what the cipher means?"

"I don't know, and that's the truth, Alan."

He rose from the table and flung down his napkin. "Have it your own way, then," he said, and left me to my anguished thoughts.

I sat in the living room reading—or at least trying to, for my mind was elsewhere. What was I to do? Alan needed money. Well, if I loved him, I, who was rich, could help him. But he had refused my help, saying he wanted what was his right. And that wasn't in my power to give him.

As the Swiss clock chimed ten, he came into the living room, wearing his hat and coat, and said, "I'm going out for a drive. I'm all worked up about this mess, Arlene."

"As you wish, Alan. But I've told you I'll give you the money you need. Won't you be satisfied with that and with my love?"

"And I told you I want what's rightfully mine, my legacy from my grandfather, just as you had yours from your family. That's simple enough. I'm going now."

Without another word, he left the house, slamming the door behind him. I had to fight the tears as I rose and walked to the kitchen. A glass of hot milk and a sleeping pill would give me deep, restful sleep and let me escape from the dark shadows Alan Caswell had summoned.

I slept, yes, but once again my restless, agitated thoughts overcame the soporific, and I came gradually awake to hear once again that curious clinking sound from the distance, muffled and clandestine. And then, all around me, the darkness was shattered by that unearthly sound of moaning and of the lapping of the waves. And once again Alan's place beside me in the bed was empty. With all my power of will, I kept from crying out his name, as I had done that other night. And at last there was silence as the dense fog from the ocean shrouded the entire house, hiding even the first glint of dawn.

Chapter
TWENTY

THE FOG had not lifted even by midmorning, and when I woke and drew back the curtains, I saw how isolated and lost the old house was. As I was too, now, for there could be little left of a marriage where there was mistrust and suspicion.

Alan had not returned, but Rosie told me that he had just phoned to say that he had spent the night at his club so as to get an early start for a meeting with a client in San Rafael and that he would be home for dinner. I hunted through the house for the book in which John Dade had written that mystifying cipher about the *Afrikander*'s treasure, but there was no sign of it. He must have hidden it far more carefully than I or else taken it with him. And that he had had no right to do.

Why hadn't he been as honest with me in this as he had been at the very start of our relationship? Or had he been playing a part, an actor cunningly fortified in advance with his lines that would win me, a trusting Juliet, to him, not Romeo but Iago? I, who had thought myself such a judge of people, having myself known the guise and play-acting of the stage, now began to doubt even myself.

And then, at noon, the phone rang and I hastened to it, hoping that it might be Alan, calling to apologize for his cruel words. I had made up my mind to prove my fidelity and love for him; I was going to tell him that I'd help him find that treasure—if, indeed, it really existed after all these years.

But it was Ron Jennings instead, excited and impatient to tell me what he had just found out. "I finally worked it out, Arlene!" he exclaimed. "Your grandfather just reversed the Morse code, so that the first letter is the last, the second the next to last, and so on. I've written it down—I stayed up most of the night and just now got it all to the last word. Can I see you?"

"Of course, Ron. I'm alone except for my maid."

"Good!" He chuckled. "To tell you the honest truth, I needed a little vacation. My muscles have been getting stiff with all that heavy unloading down at the docks, so this was a great mental workout. I'll be right over, Arlene."

Half an hour later, I let him in. He wasn't dressed like a dock hand this time but was as neatly groomed in a pinstripe worsted suit as Alan himself. "I'd have been here earlier, but it was hard to find a cab. I've never seen such a spell of fog, Arlene. And the weather reports say it's going to stick around till at least tomorrow morning."

As I had opened the door to admit him, I had seen the curling wreaths of fog blanketing the housetops. A car went by, creeping slowly, its headlights dimmed by that obscuring haze. And the air was damp and chilly.

I called to Rosie to bring us some coffee, and then we sat down on the living-room couch as he took a typed sheet of paper out of his coat pocket and handed it to me.

I have salvaged the *Afrikander* treasure, the strongbox with gold and jewels. There were no survivors. I brought men from the north who are not known to our San Francisco seamen, and I paid them well to find the box, but I did not open it before them. I shall bury it under the last stone step in the cellar and leave it there, either for myself if my fortunes decline—and Henry Caswell has done his best by dishonest speculation and conniving with our competitors to bring that about—or for my descendants. Let this cipher be as binding as my will, with the stipulation that the contents of this box must go only to a Dade.

And there followed my grandfather's name and the date of the cipher, March 11, 1904.

"So it's here in this very house," he said, "and I'll bet it all that your husband's after it."

"Yes, he's said as much. And he said it belonged to him as his legacy from his grandfather. Ron, I'm afraid. There have been strange things going on."

He took my hand in his. "Tell me what they are. Because I want to help."

"I wonder . . ." I began. And then, seeing his steady look and remembering how his father had been kind to my own lonely father in the latter's isolated childhood, I knew that I could have no secrets from Ron Jennings. And I told him of the strange clinking noises and of the moaning and the lapping of water and Alan's strange absences at those times. And finally, I told him how Aunt Clara had quarreled with Alan just before she died.

He listened gravely. And when I had finished, he said, "I want you to trust me, Arlene. I'm not going to frighten you by saying what I think, but I want to stay here tonight. I could hide in the attic."

"Hide? But why?"

"To hear those sounds. To find out why they're being made—and what's making them. Will you let me?" His hand had tightened over mine till I winced with pain. And it frightened me, that intensity of his, and so I faltered, "Yes, Ron. But he mustn't find you. I don't want you to endanger yourself."

He looked at me, then said very quietly, "That goes double for you, and that's why I want to be around. Now show me where the attic is."

Alan and I had finished dinner, and Rosie had cleared away the dishes and was busy in the kitchen. My husband had been in a most congenial mood, as if nothing had happened between us. At his suggestion, to which I at once acquiesced, we played cribbage for an hour or two, and when the game was over, he got up, came over to me and kissed me, and said, "You look tired and drawn, darling. I'm sorry. I've been bullying you, and I didn't mean to. I think I know how to get the money I need, and it won't come from you. Things are going to be better."

"I'm glad, Alan. Can't we leave this gloomy old house? I think I'd so much rather live in that apartment of yours."

He kissed me again. "It's long rented by now, darling. There'll be another place, just as nice—you'll see. Now what do you say to drinking your milk like a good girl and then getting a good night's sleep?"

"All right. I am a little tired."

"I'll get the milk myself. I'm sure Rosie's on her way to bed by now." Again he kissed me, then left the room. I went back to the bedroom and began to undress, nervous and ill at ease. Perhaps I had completely misjudged him. If he were threatened with financial ruin, that would explain his preoccupation, his avoidance of me, his feverish desire to straighten things out by himself. And that was what had strained things between us.

Yet those unearthly sounds and his absence late at night—what did they mean? And why had Ron Jennings seemed so insistent in asking to hide in the house tonight?

"Here you are, darling." Alan had returned with my glass of milk.

"Thanks, Alan dear. I—I'm sorry if I've been unreasonable and nasty." I set the glass down on the night table.

"When this is all over, Arlene, we'll go away on a nice long vacation. Maybe to Hawaii, for a second honeymoon. Would you like that?"

"Oh, very much, Alan."

He took me in his arms and kissed me again. "We'll see. Now I'll get ready for bed and be back in a jiffy. And we'll both get a good night's sleep. You drink your milk like a good girl."

"I will."

But as soon as he had left the room, I took the glass and stared at it. Was it my imagination that it seemed murkier and thicker than milk usually looks? Had Ron Jennings' unspoken concern caused me to fear everything Alan did? Whatever the reason, I went quickly to the bathroom and poured nearly all of it down the washbasin and ran the tap to hide the evidence. Then I went back to bed, setting the glass back down on the night table with perhaps an inch or two of its contents left. And drawing the covers about me, I closed my eyes and feigned sleep. . . .

I don't know how long it was, perhaps an hour, perhaps more, but I felt the bed shift as Alan stealthily clambered out. He stood for a moment watching me, and I felt my heart pound violently as I strove to keep up my pretense of sleep and regular breathing. Then at last, as if satisfied, he stooped to put on his slippers and his robe and left the bedroom, opening the door and leaving it wide. I waited, and the silence grew oppressive. And then I heard the distant clinking, and as it dwindled for a moment, the room was filled with the sound of that hideous moan.

I got out of bed, put on my robe and slippers, and went slowly down the corridor. The clinking sound seemed louder now as I went into the kitchen, and I knew at last that it came from the cellar. Turning on the pantry light, I went down the rickety flight of steps to the landing, and then I stopped, a hand to my mouth.

Alan Caswell was standing with his back to me, a pickax in his right hand. With an oath, he attacked the stone at the bottom step of those five stairs which led to the bolted door and in turn to the garden. I knew now that he had deciphered that puzzling code. I knew now what had made that clinking sound all these brooding, lonely, terrifying nights.

He hadn't heard me, and I shrank back into the shadow of the narrow old wooden stairway. It was fortunate that I did so, for at that moment he half-turned, and I caught sight for a fleeting instant of his face—unrecognizably shadowed and contorted, his eyes glittering and narrowed. Then he moved to the right and crouched down over what looked like an instrument panel set in a small rectangular box.

He chuckled softly to himself, and as he did so, I heard the same blood-curdling moan that had filled me with terror in our bedroom in the dead of night. Now I knew his malevolence; he had utilized some kind of tape recording to pipe those ghastly sounds into the bedroom. And then, as I listened, trembling with incredulity and despair at my husband's treachery, he touched another button on the panel, and once again the lapping of waves was heard.

He touched another button, and there was silence again. Rising, he chuckled. "Very effective," he said to himself. "Perfect for hallucinations. But poor Arlene won't need them now. Not with all those sleeping pills in her milk. The strain of losing her aunt was just too much, so she took the easy way out."

"And what way will you take, Alan?" I said aloud.

He uttered an oath, whirled, and took a step forward, staring at me. "But you drank the milk," he accused. "You can't possibly be still alive! Damn you!"

"No, Alan, I didn't drink it. I poured it down

the washbasin so that you'd think I drank it. And I pretended to have fallen asleep till you left the bed. And I followed those sounds."

"So you were clever," he said, sneering. "But that isn't going to stop me. That treasure buried under this step belonged to my grandfather. And now it's going to belong to me. John Dade should have turned it in to the company for equal shares, but he wanted it all for himself. Well, you don't need it, not with your half-a-million-dollar trust fund and all the stock in your fine company!"

Now, at last, there was no more evasiveness between us. Now I could face him, without fear—yes, and without love. Because I could see that it had all been pretense and that I had had only myself to blame for having stubbornly refused to believe that this charming, suave, personable young man could have been warped by the twisted obsession of the past. He had been a far more cunning play-actor than I, but now the play was over.

"I told you once before, Alan," I said calmly, "that I was willing to help you out of your financial difficulties. That's what a wife's for. And since you feel that way, take this treasure, whatever it may be. You schemed to get it, and you've earned it."

He looked at me, and then he began to laugh, and his handsome face was cruel now with a kind of sneering triumph, as if he had proved how superior he was and how markedly inadequate I had been in the face of his cunning.

"Of course I've earned it, you little fool," he told me. "And it wasn't easy. But what can you know of planning and waiting and then seizing the opportunity when it comes after all these years? You, who had everything handed to you on a silver platter since the very day you were born!"

"Then you never loved me?" I could speak dispassionately now, since there was nothing more to lose and surely nothing to gain. I could speak to him with a calm contempt, a contempt that was partly from my own contrariness in defying Aunt Clara's warnings. Yes, I had been so sure that I knew Alan Caswell and that he was the man for me. Yet not only had he deceived me from the start, but now he could tell me that the scheme had been laid long before I even knew that he existed.

"Oh, these few months with you were pleasant enough, Arlene—I won't deny you that. You're not too bad-looking, and you do have money and a company to your credit. But if you want to know the truth, and you may as well now, my father told me a long time ago, when I was a little boy, that I must never forget how John Dade cheated his father out of his rightful due and even drove him to his death."

"And you believed such a hateful lie and lived with it all these years. You, whom I took to be so sophisticated and worldly and wise, to be taken in by what you accepted so easily as gospel truth!"

His face contorted with fury, and he came toward me, drawing back his fist as if to strike me. I stood my ground and faced him with a cold defiance. "Go ahead," I told him, "because that will be the final truth that this was all a lie. I have it coming. I believed you. I loved you. I loved you until now, because I thought that your anxiety over money had changed you from the thoughtful and tender husband that you were to me in Hawaii."

He shrugged with a sneering smile and let his hand open and fall to his side. "I don't intend to strike you or to leave any marks that would be found on you and cause suspicion, dear Arlene." His voice was taunting. "It's a pity you didn't drink that milk, because then everything would have been so simple for you. I am afraid I am going to have to arrange an accident for you—though, of course, out of tender sentiment for the happy hours we did share, I can offer you the alternative of drinking a glass of milk in front of me this time. It will be painless. Sleeping pills generally are."

"Then you intend to kill me?"

"I'm afraid I'll have to now. You see, there's more than just this hidden treasure that I'm after. I want to be a part of the Dade Navigation Company, too. And once you're out of the way, Henry Pitt and I will have a chance to run it as it ought to be run. Women don't belong in business, not just by right of inheritance. And that'll make up to me for what John Dade did to my grandfather. That's even better than the treasure."

"Then it was you I saw with Henry Pitt that afternoon when I came out of the Ferry Building, Alan?" I knew that I was goading him perhaps beyond his control, but having gone so far I had to know all the answers to this horrid travesty which had been our marriage.

"Of course. What you couldn't be expected to know was that your two top executives in the company, Henry Pitt and William Pearson, were jealous of each other. And Henry Pitt always had a secret ambition to be more than just the general manager. As long as you and your aunt were alive, there wasn't much he could do about it. So when I read in the papers that you'd come into your fortune and that lovely block of preferred stock, I made up my mind to have a try at making you fall in love with me. It was really very easy."

"Thank you for the compliment. Then you must have gone out of your way to arrange to meet me so that you could put your romantic technique to work, I suppose?"

"That was rather a neat touch, wasn't it, my dear?" Alan smirked, and his shoulders seemed to straighten with a boastful pride. "All I had to do was follow you about and wait for the opportune moment. I have a friend who's not a bad actor himself, you see. We followed you downtown that day, and I was in a cab while my friend took your purse away from you."

"So even that heroic rescue of a lady in distress was part of your little plan? I congratulate you, Alan."

"Thank you, my dear. Then, once I'd made myself attractive enough to you to let you become my wife, I paid a visit to the offices of your company. My visit was in the nature of a courtesy call, of course, so I could feel out both Pitt and Pearson. And your ambitious general manager went for the bait hook, line, and sinker. He intimated that he would be very grateful to me if somehow I could persuade you to sell your preferred stock or in some other way dispose of the company so that he could get full control. Of course, there was your aunt as a rather difficult obstacle, because she could stand to inherit from you if anything should happen to you."

I was almost numb with horror as he glibly and boastfully revealed the insidious steps in his path to vengeance over the Dades. But I forced myself to ask him a final question. "How did you kill Aunt Clara, Alan? Tell me that."

He lit a cigarette, inhaled savoringly, and then blew out a wreath of blue smoke, raising his eyes to watch it ascend toward the ceiling of this cellar which had become the final stage of this masque of mockery and sham and even murder. "She didn't suffer, Arlene. With asthma and a heart condition, all you really need is a pillow gently applied over the nose and mouth. There wasn't any struggle, and I'm sure Doctor Hargrove was satisfied or he wouldn't have signed the death certificate." He took a puff of his cigarette, smiled mockingly at me, then added, "And now that you know all this, you certainly don't expect me to let you go on living very much longer, do you, my sweet? I think you'd better settle for the glass of milk. Come—we'll go to the kitchen and I'll prepare it for you. And then you'll go back to bed and close your eyes and go to sleep. It's really the easiest way. I'm rather fond of you in a way, and I'd much prefer it to happen like this rather than to contrive an accident. That would be painful."

"I'm afraid you'll have to use your ingenuity, Alan. I won't help you any more, but I'm not afraid. I wonder if you have the stamina to kill me in cold blood."

"Damn you to hell, yes, I have! You're the only one that stands between me and what I've always dreamed of having, of being! I'm going to carry you up to the attic and push you out of the window. I'm sure you'll break your pretty neck. And I've already told Doctor Hargrove several times the past few weeks how distraught you've been. He'll put it down to suicide. And now I've finished with talking."

He seized my wrists with his right hand, clapping his left over my mouth, and attempted to drag me up the rickety wooden stairs. I struggled and, with desperate effort, sank my teeth into his palm. He released me with a violent oath and then struck me with his fist, and I stumbled to the floor, on my hands and knees before him. He stared at me with a savage and implacable hatred now, and then he tore away the belt of his bathrobe and grasped me, preparing to bind my wrists. I screamed aloud, and then I heard Alan utter another oath, and suddenly I was free.

Ron Jennings had come down the steps. Alan rushed back toward the stone steps and retrieved the pickax, then turned to meet the young dock hand. Ron flung himself forward and hurled Alan back against the damp stone wall.

The pickax clattered to the floor, and Alan, with a groan, slumped against Ron. The force of Ron's charge had driven my husband's head against the sharp angle of the stone wall, and I saw blood upon the corner.

Ron lowered my husband's sagging body to the floor, his left arm supporting Alan's shoulders, his right hand feeling for the heartbeat. And then he looked up at me, his handsome young face taut with an agony of compassion. "He's dead, Arlene. I didn't mean to kill him. I wanted the law to punish him for what he did to you. I heard what he told you—yes, all of it. How he murdered your aunt. All I wanted to do was to knock him out and then get the police."

"Again you saved my life, Ron." My voice was tremblingly uneven as I fought for control, for I was very close to hysteria now. "And in a way, it was best this way, for him. He'd have gone to the gas chamber for murdering Aunt Clara, and there would have been all the newspaper publicity and the notoriety and the destruction of all that pride of his and that ambition. And all because he wanted to believe in vengeance without caring that perhaps his grandfather had been altogether in the wrong. Call the police, Ron. It's over now."

"I hate to think of your being involved in something like this, Arlene. There'll be scandal and publicity for you now, you know that."

"It's a small price to pay, Ron, for what my own blind sentimentality allowed to happen. If I hadn't married Alan, Aunt Clara would be alive today. I shall have to live with that knowledge all the rest of my life. Now call the police."

It is November now, and the rain and the fog have their way with the house on Union Street. The statement I made to the police, corroborated by Ron Jennings, was accepted by the district attorney. For a great deal of further evidence came to light as soon as the news of Alan Caswell's death was printed. The private investigator whom my aunt had engaged to check on Alan's possible extracurricular marital activities called me that very day and went with me to the district attorney's office to produce a report that showed that Alan Caswell had been involved with Ellen Wilbur, who had been his sweetheart for a year prior to our seemingly dramatic meeting. And when Ellen Wilbur was subpoenaed, she tearfully admitted that my husband had told her that he eventually intended to marry her as soon as he could bring off a business coup that would make him rich for life.

I promoted William Pearson to the post of general manager of the Dade Navigation Company after Henry Pitt had voluntarily submitted his resignation to me and thrown himself upon my mercy. I had no desire to prosecute him. He had certainly never contemplated murder; that had been Alan Caswell's idea as the speediest way to bring off that intended "coup." His life was ruined, and his own ambition was thus forever ended; that would be punishment enough for Henry Pitt.

I have seen to it that Ron Jennings will be offered a tempting position—though at first in a minor executive capacity—in the Dade Navigation Company. I can foresee that he will rise swiftly to the post that William Pearson formerly held. He loves the sea and the shipping business, and he has a good mind, and he is not warped by ruthless ambition. Nor will his alert integrity be diminished by changing his sphere of operations from the docks to the office in the Ferry Building.

The treasure? Yes, it was there, as John Dade's cipher said it would be. Gold coins and jewels, which experts have appraised at a value of well over a hundred thousand dollars. I have given it to charities and to clinical research in Aunt Clara's name.

The old house on Union Street is lonelier than ever now, with just myself and Rosie and an occasional visit from garrulous old Henry Jennings. When the fog shrouds it, as it does at this very moment as I write these final lines, I feel myself isolated from all the rest of the world. It is a kind of penance for me. Ron Jennings has told me that after a while, when all the notoriety of the newspaper stories about Alan has been forgotten, he would like to pay his respects to a girl whom he happens to be very fond of, and I have told him that he must wait until I am wiser. Wiser in learning that love does not come entirely out of romantic idealization as it did with Jim Kinsolving. Nor out of infatuation and a kind of proud defiance, as it did with Alan Caswell. And least of all, not out of gratitude.

It would be easy to fall in love with Ron Jennings for that last reason, when I consider that he twice saved my life. But I must do my penance first before I can be worthy of his love. And when the time is meant for us to come together, if it is so meant, both of us must come together free of ties from the past.

Once he is settled in his work and certain that it is through his own merit that he achieves what I know he will achieve in the company my father left to me, and once I can put aside the emotional obligations under which his courage and his alertness placed me, then perhaps one day we can meet as two persons who can build a purposeful and happy life together.

The fog that covers the city is at times depressing, and at times it hides the fury of unsuspected violence and treacherous undertakings. But we who love the city that defied earthquake and fire to come to a glorious rebirth of beauty and life and spirit and hope—we know that even its thickest and most obscuring fogs will ultimately vanish when the sun and the free wind and the dazzling blue of sky and ocean so command.

LOOK FOR OUR MAGNUM CLASSICS